Christmas at Cherry Bounce Inn

A Demeter Society Story

BOOK 3

Books in the Demeter Society Series
by Amanda Schwantes
Enjoy as a series or read as stand-alones

Cedar Hollow Farm: Book 1
The Midwest Farmer's Guide to Love: Book 2
Christmas at Cherry Bounce Inn: Book 3

For EMF

The heart has its reasons of which reason knows nothing...We know the truth not only by the reason, but by the heart.

-Blaise Pascal

Chapter One

In Which the Holiday Season
Commences With a Splash

Although she wouldn't describe her current mood as actually Scrooge-like, Lindsay definitely lacked that spark of holiday spirit that began kindling in the breasts of even the most stoic inhabitants of Namur, Wisconsin after the first snow of winter. She did have a lot on her mind after all, not the least of which was how to get her inn ready for the guest who would be arriving in a matter of hours and had been an unsatisfied customer during every one of her previous seven stays.

No. Unsatisfied was putting it too mildly. Mrs. Johnston was an aggressively disgruntled customer with an active account on every review site that specialized in travel accommodations, bed and breakfasts, and agritourism-every one that Lindsay was familiar with, anyway.

It wasn't that Lindsay hadn't done her best to make Mrs. Johnston's annual Christmastime stay at

Cherry Bounce Inn joyous, lovely, and comfortable. In fact, Lindsay herself would go so far as to say that she had gone above and beyond every single time. And every single time, without fail, something was found wanting.

Two years ago, to pick a recent example, Mrs. Johnston had complained that the bedroom floors were too cold in the morning. That should've been a simple fix. Lindsay added a plush rug to the room. The following year, however, Mrs. Johnston decried the rug as being too slippery, accusing the person who had positioned it next to the bed of "harboring a nefarious plot to break the necks of her unsuspecting lodgers." Lindsay was nonplussed. She tried sliding on the rug, but it wouldn't budge an inch, due to the rubber webbing holding it in place.

Earlier this morning, Lindsay had stood in the middle of their best guest room and agonized over that rug. Should she remove it or leave it there? No one else had complained, but as far as Mrs. Johnston was concerned, cold feet would probably be preferable to a broken neck. Lindsay removed the rug and carried it off to her room, where it would stay for the duration of her lodger's one night stay.

Of all the things Lindsay had to worry about this year however, having a white Christmas wasn't going to be one of them. It was only December 8th and six inches of powder, left behind by the first big storm of winter, coated the viburnum hedge outside her window.

Lindsay cracked open the cupboard and peeked

in on her molasses bread dough, which had been left to rise for a couple of hours. She'd developed a theory, untested but seemingly sound, that bread rose faster in the cupboard than it did out on the counter, where the chill of the inn in the early morning could slow its rise considerably. Why the cupboard would be any warmer than the rest of the kitchen, positioned as it was next to an outer wall, she couldn't say, but it seemed cozier in there somehow, more snug for the shiny lump of nascent bread. And look at that, the towel covering the glass bowl was mounded in the middle already, the dough beneath it ready to scoop out and form into two rustic loaves.

Lindsay floured the counter, turned out the dough, and split the ball in two. As she folded the halves over, tucking under their edges, she called up to Grace, "Is Mrs. Johnston's room ready?"

Her sister bounded down the stairs, pausing in the middle. "Just about, but I'm giving it an extra scouring. Do we have any of those chocolate mints to put on her pillow?"

"Umm...I'm not sure." Lindsay was sure. In an effort to cut corners-or economize, as she preferred to call it in her more optimistic moments-she'd foregone her customary trip to Door County Confectionary. It wasn't just the lodgers who were missing out, though. Lindsay sorely missed her traditional Christmas box of chocolate angel food. Maybe next year...

"That's okay, I'll look later." Grace disappeared back upstairs.

Lindsay scored a tic-tac-toe pattern in the top

of the bread and plopped both loaves onto a cornmeal dusted cookie sheet. They'd rise a while longer before going into the oven. A quarter sized dollop of dough stuck to the side of the bowl. Lindsay peeled it away with a finger and popped it into her mouth. Yeasty, with just a tang of ginger. Perfection.

What else needed to be done before their guest arrived in two hours? "BEEP, BEEP, BEEP." An alarm screeched in the basement, the one that was supposed to alert her to water on the floor. Lindsay hurried to the source of the sound, tightness building in her chest. This couldn't have come at a worse time, although it was likely a random little drip of condensation or something. That sensor was always on the fritz, but she hated to get rid of it, afraid that the moment she did she'd set off an aquatic catastrophe down there and have no one but herself to blame.

Reaching the basement in record time, Lindsay surveyed the scene. It hadn't been a false alarm after all, and it wasn't an encouraging sight. The sensor wasn't in its usual helpful position near the pipes that led to the well. It leaned against the far wall instead, blissfully unaware of the deluge. Thanks to its position, well away from any possible source of a leak, it wasn't going to panic until water had pooled far and wide throughout the room, much like it was doing at that inconvenient instant.

This couldn't be happening. Not now. Lindsay shook the water off the sensor, but it continued shrieking in her hand. Her ears bore the brunt of its warning call. She sprinted to the side wall, where a

Tupperware full of summer clothes perched on a tall wooden shelf. Yanking open the lid, Lindsay wedged the sensor inside before going back to assess the damage. The sensor carried on, more quietly now, in the dark amongst the hibernating sundresses and t-shirts.

With her ears still ringing, Lindsay returned to the source of the problem, where water sprayed from the main pipe leading into the house. What to do? She scanned the tangle of pipes, eyeing up various levers and knobs. Harvey had shown her what to do in a situation like this, but Lindsay couldn't remember which valve shut off the water that ran from the well to the house.

That red plastic handle looked promising... Lindsay pushed it from right to left. Nope. The steady mist showed no sign of slowing. She tried to turn a rusty knob near the ceiling, but it wouldn't budge. There was nothing else for it. The well pump would have to be disconnected at the electrical box.

"Lindsay? Are you down there? Mrs. Johnston just called to say she'd be here early..." Grace gasped when she reached the scene of the calamity. "What happened?"

"The pipe sprung a leak. Can you grab some towels?"

Grace sprinted away without another word while Lindsay strode over to the electrical panel. She flipped the breaker to shut off the well's pump. The bare bulbs hanging from the ceiling flickered out. Shoot. She'd hit the wrong switch. In pitch darkness now, Lindsay ran her hand over the electrical panel. All the switches felt like identical plastic knobs. It was like playing Memory in the dark when she hadn't flipped a card in six months.

A wedge of light came from upstairs. "Why are the lights out?" Grace called down into the pitch blackness.

"I was trying to turn off the well pump and hit the wrong breaker. Can you grab a flashlight?"

"On it."

Lindsay put her hand over her heart and took a deep breath. She was going to be alright. She and Grace would sort this out. Her shirt was clammy and wet from the spraying water. Spots of light sprang up in her vision as her eyes struggled to adjust to the darkness.

Soon, a real light bobbed towards her, followed by her little sister. Newly armed with the flashlight, a very wet innkeeper flipped the basement lights back on and chose a different breaker, keeping her fingers crossed this time. It worked. The humming of the well stopped; the spraying water gradually slowed.

All the towels Grace and Lindsay could find were just enough to mop up the puddles. They saved one for their persnickety guest, however, who probably wouldn't appreciate having to towel off with basement floor water.

Just as they were blotting up the last of the mess, the doorbell rang. It couldn't possibly be Mrs. Johnston already, could it? Lindsay raced upstairs, a single strand of curly chestnut hair plastered to her forehead. The see-through nature of her wet shirt exposed a fun polka dot bra that she'd chosen that morning as an antidote to a potentially difficult day.

Lindsay, panting and disheveled, flung open the door to reveal that not only could it be Mrs. Johnston, but it was. She stood on the stoop two hours early and as haughty and pointy nosed as ever. Her sneer, which had already been prepared especially for Lindsay, was joined by a downturned mouth and an upward tilt of the head as she took in her hostess's appearance. Here was a woman with an eye that could fry an egg at fifty paces and was aiming that eye directly at Lindsay, who would've benefitted from a much fuzzier gaze.

"Have I come at a bad time?" the ill-tempered lodger asked. She raised one eyebrow and then the other, and Lindsay was one part impressed, one part tempted to slide them back into place with both of her waterlogged pointer fingers, an impulse she wisely resisted.

Instead, she put on her cheeriest smile and said, "You've come at a perfect time. We've just had a little mishap in the basement, but I assure you..."

"A mishap? I don't like the sound of that, not at all. Please tell me if I should take my business elsewhere, and I will happily do so." She pivoted as if prepared to leave.

"It won't affect the quality of your stay in any way."

Mrs. Johnston snorted, her expression an odd mixture of disapproval and elation. "I'll take your word for it," she said, but her tone communicated something that sounded a whole lot more like "Says you."

"Wonderful. Please come in. I'll show you to your room." Lindsay hefted two bulky suitcases through the kitchen and up the narrow staircase to their very best guest room, the largest one that overlooked the rustic barn, snow covered fields, and sturdy northern forest beyond. Lindsay set the luggage on the polished floor and smoothed out an intricate patchwork quilt. The mirror above the dresser shone; the antique lamp on the nightstand was lit, illuminating a portrait of her great-grandmother with a turtledove, and the pillow on the old wooden rocker was fluffed. So far, so good. Everything was going to be fine.

"I'm going to run to the ladies' room," said Mrs. Johnston.

"Be my guest. Let me know if you require anything at all. Lunch will be served at noon."

Mrs. Johnston, who had already departed, slammed the bathroom door. Oh well, there was nothing Lindsay could do about it now. She'd have plenty of time to recover after she'd called the plumber. She ran downstairs, grabbed her phone off the kitchen counter, and sprinted back to the basement. The plumber's phone rang. Could he still make it over that evening? No such luck.

"I'm sorry," he said. "Unless it's really gushing, you're going to have to wait until tomorrow. I'm working on a burst pipe in an upstairs bathroom in town. Your basement isn't finished, is it?"

Lindsay glanced around. The walls were field-stone, the ceilings low and cramped. Finished? It barely qualified as started. "No, not finished."

"Alright, wrap the pipe in duct tape and turn the well back on. If that doesn't work, call me back and I'll see what I can do."

She followed his instructions to a tee. Water gathered on the outside of the duct tape and dripped into a strategically placed bucket. It wasn't ideal, but it would hold them over until the following day. Lindsay left the basement with the well humming again. Crisis averted. Mrs. Johnston would enjoy a pleasantly festive, uneventful stay, with only imaginary problems to torment her.

Lindsay continued working on lunch, humming along to Jingle Bell Rock. She laid out a beautiful winter feast: venison stew, homemade bread, and freshly churned butter shaped like a snowflake. For dessert, there was a buche de Noel, a Belgian chocolate cake roll covered in frosting and fashioned to look like a Yule log.

Noon came and went, and Mrs. Johnston didn't show. Where could she be? During her previous stays, she'd been sure to arrive at least ten minutes early to every meal so she could complain about Lindsay's un-preparedness. Being late didn't seem to be part of her strategy. Maybe she had fallen asleep.

Not wanting to wake her, her hostess crept up the stairs. The bedroom door was open, the bed un-occupied. The fussy floral suitcases were gone, as was the fussy floral woman who had accompanied them. Lindsay was sure no one was there, but she tapped on the bathroom door nevertheless. When she didn't receive a response, she peeked inside. A message was scrawled across the mirror in bright red lipstick: *No water. Appalling.* Appalling was underlined...seven times.

Mrs. Johnston must have been overjoyed.

Lindsay wiped the mirror clean and trudged back to the kitchen. She sat at the table, looking over the feast she had prepared for nothing. While the stew could probably be reheated for lunch tomorrow, everything else would need to be made fresh. Maybe if she called Mrs. Johnston, explained what had happened...who was she kidding? If it was anyone else, she would've reached out, but the effort would be wasted on this particular guest.

Grace came up from the basement to find Lindsay digging into the dessert.

"Umm...don't you think we should save that for our lodger?"

"Nope." Lindsay shoveled another forkful into her mouth.

"I feel like I'm missing something. Where's Mrs. Johnston?"

"Gone."

"Gone?" Grace crossed the kitchen and plucked the utensil out of Lindsay's hand. Not to be deterred, Lindsay stared ahead in a daze and dipped her finger in the cream filling, licking it off with a flourish. She had officially given up for the day.

"Are you going to fill me in?" Grace asked. "Because you're kind of freaking me out." She licked the fork. "This is really good. I'm having some too, if that's where this afternoon is taking us."

Grace handed the fork back to Lindsay and grabbed one of her own. They sat there with their cake roll and ate a while until Lindsay decided she was ready to share the bad news.

"That's not great," said Grace, when her sister finished the story with an account of the lipstick covered mirror, "but she was going to give us bad reviews anyway. Good riddance, I say."

"Her money walked out the door with her, though."

Grace shrugged. "She was only staying one night. We're booked the rest of the month. One night is nothing."

One night was not nothing, as they were both well aware, but Lindsay appreciated her sister's attempt to find the silver lining. She'd try to do the same. She got another bowl from the cupboard and filled it with the delicious stew she'd woken up early to prepare.

"You know what?" said Grace, taking a deep sniff of the hearty venison and carrots in her bowl. "This was probably meant to be. That woman has been coming here for years just to sneer at us. You could've denied her a reservation. Why did you let her keep coming back, anyway?" She slathered a chunk of bread with butter and dipped it into the rich broth.

"That's a good question. I suppose I thought I could win her over. But yes, you're right, it's probably better for us that she's not coming back."

"I won't be at all surprised if she calls again next year."

"Me either." Lindsay took a bite of stew. It was perfect: salty, peppery, and rich, with just the right amount of rosemary.

"You know what else is kind of nice about this? We can go get our tree this afternoon and set it up when we get back. It'll be all ready for when that group comes tomorrow afternoon."

"That group, right. Something seemed off about them, too. They'll be staying here for three weeks straight though, so I didn't ask any questions."

Grace paused, her spoon halfway to her mouth. "You didn't say anything about potential weirdness."

"It's nothing, really. The guy who called was a really intense loud-talker. I had to turn the volume all the way down on my phone before I could hold it to my ear. It was like he was giving a campaign speech into his microphone. He asked if we had any trail cameras set up in the orchard. Said he was interested in the local wildlife."

"Do we?"

Lindsay took another bite and shook her head. "Just one. I put it up in the orchard last summer. It doesn't work at night though, so it's not particularly useful. He asked if he could install some to use while he was here. I told him that was fine. I wonder what he's looking for."

"Deer, most likely, and if that's the case, he won't be disappointed. I've been seeing quite a few of them in the orchard in the morning on my way to work."

"Yeah. You're probably right." Lindsay wasn't so sure, though. She couldn't say what it was exactly, but she had a sinking feeling that their next guests were going to be full of surprises. Whether those surprises were something to be desired remained to be seen, but given how the rest of the year had been shaping up, Lindsay somehow doubted it.

After lunch, Grace ran upstairs to put on some makeup while Lindsay bundled up in her jacket, hat, and mittens. On her way outside, she almost tripped over a present that had been left on the top step.

She picked it up and lifted the tag. It had her name on it. Who would've left her a gift? There were so many tire tracks and footprints in the snow that they weren't revealing any secrets, so she gave the box a little shake, brought it inside, and set it on the table.

"Ooh, for me?" Grace asked when she came into the kitchen. She picked it up, giving it a shake.

"I guess it's for me," said Lindsay.

"Who's it from? Did someone just drop it off?"

"It was on the porch. There's no note."

"Well, open it already. The suspense is killing me."

Lindsay hesitated for a moment.

"It's probably one of your friends bringing you some extra cheer," Grace reassured her. "They know we're in need of it."

"You're probably right." Lindsay resisted the urge to pick it up and listen for a ticking sound. Instead, she tore off the paper and popped the lid. A lovely old ornament nestled among soft white tissue. The silvery blue globe shimmered in the light above them, a sparkly poinsettia on one side and Merry Christmas on the other.

"It's gorgeous," said Grace. "Lucky we're going to get our perfect tree today. We can put it up front and center."

Lindsay set the ornament back into the tissue and left it on the table. Whoever made the delivery must've known her well enough to be aware that she collected antique ornaments. Grace was right. It was likely one of her friends, one of the women from the Demeter Society. It was such a small thing, but it made her day to know that someone had been thinking of her and surprised her like that.

The ice that had threatened to encase her heart completely was tapped by a little pickaxe, creating cracks that would let in some warmth. She had some hope that there would be bright spots amongst the challenges of this holiday season.

Chapter Two

*In Which a Silent Night is Interrupted
by an Intruder*

Lindsay sniffled and slapped her mittened hands together. Instead of crumbling to the ground as intended, snow caked into thin alpaca wool grooves, sealing her numb fingered fate. Brushing away the downy snowflakes on her bobble hat, she tipped her face to the sky where the wind, sifting down from the North Pole and blustering across the Great Lakes, buffeted along a couple of vagrant white clouds.

"Hurry up," Grace called over her shoulder. "So many trees, so little time."

"Didn't you say we'd be home before it got dark?" The sun, whose greatest height had come and gone hours ago, was sinking in the western sky.

"I said we'd be home by dinner. Should've mentioned I've been eating late."

Lindsay's stomach grumbled.

"Quit complaining," said Grace.

Alright, that was the last straw. Lindsay packed together a clump of snow. Grace's sleek belted parka was just within throwing range. A little closer and she would be right where Lindsay wanted her.

This wasn't vindictive, by the way. It was tradition. Item eleven on Grace's holiday master list clearly stated: *Christmas Tree Hunt Snowball Fight*. Would Lindsay get extra satisfaction from pelting the indecisive tree inspector with a well-aimed snowball? Sure. Would she have done it even without the tradition? Of course, but Grace didn't need to know that.

Lindsay took aim. Bonus points for landing it in that fuzzy fur trimmed hood. It was now or never... The snowball arced through the air and landed with a plop halfway between them. Who was she kidding? She couldn't fake it today, having expended all of her effort just to act enthused about their epic hunt.

In a normal year, Lindsay would be just as raring to break out the eggnog and fire up the Yuletide music after the first of December as the next owner of an adorable and well-appointed bed and breakfast. Today, however, after the basement water debacle, she marched forward robotically, one foot in front of the other. Her sister was even farther up ahead now, giving another tree the old once-over and then shaking her head, apparently finding it wanting.

"Can we just pick one? Please? My hands and feet are going numb," said Lindsay.

Grace looked at her as though she'd just suggested they hop in the car and head on over to the nearest big box store so they could grab the first pre-decorated representative of the evergreen family they came across. Horrific. "Just pick one, you say? No way. It's my first year living back home in ages, and this is going to be our official tree."

"What about that one back there somewhere?" Lindsay pointed vaguely in the direction from whence they'd come. All the trees were starting to look the same.

"That one was a little sparse in the back."

"No one will be able to tell. That side will be facing the wall."

"No, but I'll know."

Lindsay had no argument for that logic. It was true. Grace would be haunted by that terrible knowledge.

Lindsay marched forward and bumped into a snowy fir; a cascade of snow rained into the neck of her down jacket. She shrieked, shimmying her shoulders to slough the icy crystals down her back. It didn't work. They stuck to her and started to melt.

If Grace wondered whether her screaming sister had fallen into a crevasse or been attacked by a yeti, nothing about her determined countenance revealed such a concern. Instead, she yelled, "Try to keep up. I think I found it."

It was the work of a moment for Lindsay to hurry over, and the work of one moment more for clammy cold water to seep down her spine and into the waistband of her jeans. The chances that this tree would be the chosen one weren't good, but they had to find an acceptable option eventually, right?

Throwing out her arms, Grace introduced their future Christmas tree with aplomb. "What do you think?" she asked.

It was at least twelve feet tall.

Lindsay eyed it up. She was tempted to let her sister down easy or even go along with it, but the trees were priced by the foot, and she couldn't afford to throw money around. She cut to the chase, shaking her head. "It's too tall. I know it seems small enough out here, but you'll be shocked at how low our ceilings look when you bring it inside."

"What do you mean? It's perfect. It even smells perfect. Look at this even branch distribution. Its form is natural without being untidy. See how the top tapers into a proud piney point?"

"It's gorgeous," Lindsay agreed, "but it's huge. We'll end up having to saw off the bottom half."

"Onward then." Grace pointed to the horizon. There was no sense in wasting time on lost opportunities while their perfect tree was still out there. She came upon another winner in minutes. "What about this one?"

Lindsay appraised the find. It passed muster: not too tall, not too wide, not a sparse area to be seen. "I think we've found our winner," she said with false chirpiness, forcing a smile.

Picking the tree was another reminder of how much things had changed this year. This was usually the time when Lindsay would step back as Steve brandished his saw and made short work of a lovely balsam. Instead, Lindsay herself was the one who would be chopping down the tree.

She didn't mind doing it herself. In fact, she had been getting quite a bit of satisfaction from the discovery that she was capable of all kinds of things that she'd never had to do before. No, it wasn't the tasks themselves that bothered her; it was standing all alone as she did them.

Lindsay sawed away at the trunk, acting fast before her sister could change her mind. The limbs of their cherry and apple trees had provided ample practice, and she cut through it in no time. The tree flopped into the powder, and Grace lifted the top end while Lindsay took the bottom. Sharply scented sap oozed onto her wet mittens.

They stomped through the stand of trees, their boots squeaking in the snow. When they'd almost reached the garage where they would check out and have their tree wrapped, Grace asked if they could set down their quarry so she could shake out her arms and Lindsay agreed, letting it drop. Icy flakes prickled her cheeks and nose. She closed her eyes against the wind. Suddenly, a slushy projectile hit her leg with a thud. Grace had kicked off the annual snowball fight.

"Tradition eleven!" Grace shouted. So she hadn't forgotten.

Lindsay sprang into action, packing a ball of her own and flinging it at her sister's jacket. It missed, sailing over Grace's head. With a cry of triumph, Grace lobbed another snowball at her assailant before she could reload. Another hit. Lindsay spun behind a convenient spruce. Refusing to be outmaneuvered again, she threw caution to the wind, scooping up two handfuls of snow. She came out swinging. Both snowballs flew through the air, straight at their target. Grace dodged them like they were coming at her in slow motion.

"I surrender," said Lindsay, laughing. "Have you been practicing?"

"A few of the other nurses and I got really into paintball last year."

"You're kidding."

"Nope. Apparently it's amazing training for this."

Both women, rosy cheeked and beaming, gathered up their tree and marched on. They checked out with Tom, who was in his element. He wore a Santa hat and threw in a wreath as a Christmas gift. He recognized their choice of tree as one he'd always thought showed particular promise.

"See, I picked a winner again." Grace gave her sister her "I told you so" look, and Lindsay wished she had another snowball handy. Some things never changed.

"I never disputed that," said Lindsay. "Your trees are so beautiful that we couldn't decide which one to pick," she informed Tom.

He beamed. He'd retired ages ago but vowed he'd never give up his Christmas tree farm. "Why, thank you. It warms my heart to picture all the people who'll be gathering around one of my trees Christmas morning. You two enjoy it."

Lindsay and Grace thanked him and carried the tree, as well as their unexpected wreath, to the car. As they were stowing away their cargo, Chloe and Arthur pulled up next to them in Chloe's truck, Old Blue. Chloe waved frantically and hopped out.

"Hey guys," she called. "Fancy meeting you here."

Lindsay ran over and hugged her friend, whose blonde braid stuck out of a crazy striped knit hat. Arthur, Chloe's boyfriend, followed close behind.

"It's getting dark, guys," said Lindsay. "I'm pretty sure you're going to need a flashlight."

"We might just pick the first tree we come across," said Arthur. Grace gasped audibly. "I have a few on the farm that I've been pruning into Christmas trees, but I've gotten kind of attached and didn't have the heart to chop them down." He hefted his saw over his shoulder. "I'll go talk to Tom and see if he has some that are precut."

Chloe watched him walk away with a dreamy look on her face. After a moment she snapped to and said, "I just have to tell you something quick. I am so happy. I'm starting to think Arthur might be the real thing."

"I know he is," Lindsay replied. "He's adorable. Did he ask you to our big New Year's celebration yet?"

"I'm planning on asking him. Speaking of which, how's it coming along?"

"It's going well. I'm looking forward to hosting it. We haven't used the barn for an event since Halloween, and Christmas is going to be pretty quiet this year, so it'll be a bright spot for me."

"Aren't your parents coming back from Florida?"

"No," said Lindsay. "They decided not to. They're enjoying the warm weather too much. It'll just be me, Grace, and Grandma Vivian."

Chloe laughed. "If I know your grandma, it won't be all that quiet. She's a hoot. I want to be Grandma Vivian when I'm eighty."

"You're Grandma Vivian now," said Grace, who had been strolling around the trailer, checking out their new tree. It made Lindsay nervous. What if she spotted a dead branch? They weren't out of the woods yet, so to speak.

"Wow. Thank you," said Chloe. "By the way, let me know if I can do anything to help you two with the party."

"I'll take you up on that," Lindsay promised. "Your help with the Halloween party was invaluable."

"That party was great. I'm telling you, you're going to be famous for your events."

"Grace is the one who's been making them so spectacular. Before she came along, I was kind of floundering with the whole aesthetic side of things."

Chloe's eyes widened and she lowered her voice, speaking quietly enough that Grace couldn't hear her. "I just had an idea. We should ask Grace and Betsy to join the Demeter Society, now that we're each working with our sisters." Chloe's business designing ergonomic farm tools for women was taking off, and she'd just hired her sister Betsy to help keep up with its growth.

"I love it," said Lindsay. "It's about time we added some new members, and between the two of them, they probably have more energy than the rest of us put together." They smiled conspiratorially.

"What are you two whispering about?" asked Grace.

"Oh nothing," said Lindsay. "You'll find out soon enough."

"Yes, don't tell me. I love surprises."

Chloe craned her neck to see what Arthur was up to. "I'd better run, but we'll see you guys around. Are you going over to Wes's for the skating party?"

"I am," said Lindsay, "but Grace is staying home."

"Someone has to mind the inn," said Grace. "Besides, I'm hopeless on the ice. Sounds fun though."

They said their goodbyes, and Grace and Lindsay headed home with their perfect Christmas tree. They drove past the sign welcoming visitors to Cherry Bounce Inn and pulled into the drive-way. Their red brick farmhouse was always charming, but it truly shone at Christmastime. Lindsay had wrapped the columns on the front porch with real pine garlands speckled with berries. Above the porch, near the tip of the gabled roof, was a round bull's eye window surrounded by a glittering wreath. A matching wreath hung on the heavy wood-paneled main door. Artificial candles flickered in every window.

Lindsay parked in the garage, unhooked the

trailer, and rolled it out of the way. She and Grace lifted out the tree and propped it up against the barn where it would be waiting for them to decorate later that evening. Lindsay thread the wreath through her arm, and the two sisters padded up the back stairs. Lindsay stuck the key in the lock. She tried to turn it, but it wouldn't budge. That's odd. The deadbolt was already drawn back.

Lots of other people in the tiny village never locked their doors; they didn't have to. The worst thing that might befall a person was a sneaky neighbor shimmering in and leaving behind a couple of giant vegetables on the table during zucchini season, but Lindsay endorsed the old adage "better safe than sorry" and always battened down the hatches when no one was home.

"I could've sworn I locked the door behind me when we left," she said. "Or did you? Now I don't remember."

Grace shook her head. "We probably got distracted by your present and forgot."

Lindsay considered for a moment. "I can picture locking it though, because the deadbolt was a little sticky. I even pulled the door shut so I could turn it all the way."

"You think someone broke in?"

"No. I mean, not really, but...now I'm second guessing myself. It's probably fine."

Nevertheless, Lindsay pushed the door open slowly. No one waited for them in the kitchen. That was a good start. She waved Grace inside. Grace padded in behind her and tapped Lindsay on the shoulder then pointed at the crack beneath the basement door. The lights were on down there. A metallic clang echoed through the dark house. They both froze.

"Could it be the plumber?" Grace whispered.

"He couldn't have let himself in."

"Why would someone break into our house and head for the basement though? There's nothing down there. Maybe we should call the police."

"I'll feel like an idiot if it's someone we know, considering I already called them to report an arson attempt they decided didn't happen," said Lindsay.

"They didn't decide it didn't happen; there wasn't enough evidence to charge anyone. This is creepy. I've seen enough horror movies to know that if we decide it's nothing and go down there, it basically guarantees there's some kind of psycho banging around, just waiting for the curious homeowners to return."

"A psycho who bangs people's pipes? Why would he do that?"

"I don't know why psychos do what they do. That's kind of the point of them."

Grace said this as though it was very obvious, so maybe she had a point. Without removing her jacket, Lindsay set the wreath on the table then tiptoed to the cupboard and grabbed her great-grandma's cast iron pan. Armed with the pan in one hand and her phone in the other, Lindsay edged open the basement door with Grace at her heels. The lights in the stairwell were on. The two women paused to listen. More clattering and banging.

They crept down the steep uneven stairs, avoiding the ones that creaked. Pausing before they reached the final step, they looked at each other with wide eyes and pounding hearts. Lindsay pointed back up towards the safety of the kitchen. She'd changed her mind. This was a bad idea. Grace shook her head and jabbed her finger at their original destination. Apparently too close to back out now, the sisters leapt around the corner, startling Harvey. He dropped a wrench and jumped back. It clanged on the cement floor, narrowly missing his toe.

"What are you doing here?" Grace asked. Lindsay was too embarrassed to speak. She held the pan aloft, ready to knock him over the head with it. She set it down and laughed to try to ease the tension, but it came out as a croak.

"I'm so sorry," said Harvey, retrieving his wrench. "Nick called me and said you had a leaky pipe that he couldn't get to right away. I tried calling, but you didn't answer, so I left a text saying I was coming over. Then I saw that your car wasn't here, so I parked on the road so I wouldn't block the garage when you got back, and I left a note on the table and let myself in. I thought it would be a surprise but…"

He looked away, busying himself at his work bag, which slouched next to a crumpled canvas coat with flannel lining. His straight jeans were rolled at the ankle, exposing worn work boots. Lindsay would describe him as effortlessly rugged and handsome, without being aware of either. Not that she'd noticed, but if she did, that's just what she would say.

Lindsay glanced at her phone, tempted to confirm that his story checked out, but what reason would he have for lying to them? He was fixing their leaky pipe. She scolded herself for becoming so paranoid. He'd been endlessly kind to her, asking for nothing in return. She'd passed along some meals for him and his kids, which were met with adorable hand drawn thank you cards, but he'd always refused when she offered to pay him.

"I'm so sorry," she said. "I didn't get your messages. We just got home and heard noises coming from down here. We got a little freaked out." She lifted her frying pan as evidence of their concern.

"Don't apologize. I feel like I overstepped my bounds. I know you gave me the key for emergencies, but I thought it would be a mess if the leak got worse and you've got a lot on your plate..." He scratched his stubbly chin and looked away again.

This was awkward. Lindsay was actually incredibly grateful to him. If she'd gotten his call, she would have waved away his help, not wanting to be an inconvenience, but this had been a rough day, and it was comforting to know that, when she woke up in the morning, her pipe would be fixed and she could focus on the bustling weeks ahead of her.

Grace spoke up before Lindsay had a chance. "You can sneak in and fix things around here any time."

"Well," said Harvey, "your burglar's almost finished here. There were some little pinholes in the pipe between the well and the water conditioner, so I'm replacing this section. It's a really quick fix."

"You're a lifesaver. Thank you," said Lindsay. "How are James and Maddie? Are they already asleep?"

"They're in bed. James is probably still up reading, but Maddie crashes at the end of the day. You'll have to stop over soon. They were just asking about you. We're making sugar cookies Sunday night if you're interested."

The ice in Lindsay's chest melted even further. "I'd love that. Let's be in touch. We'll leave you to your work. Thanks again."

They climbed the stairs, both feeling silly. Grace pulled off her winter gear, revealing a draping cream sweater over black leggings. The leggings vanished into tall socks covered with tap dancing avocadoes in Santa hats. That was Grace for you: she came across as quite stylish and sophisticated at first glance, but stick around long enough and her dancing fruit side would show.

Grace headed into the living room while Lindsay sheepishly stowed away the frying pan and checked her phone. She had two missed calls from Harvey, a voicemail, and a text. There was also a note on the table, informing them that he was in the basement.

Before she had a chance to read it, Lindsay was interrupted by a light tap at the door. "Coming," she called. Who was stopping by now? It could be the plumber, checking in to see how Harvey was coming along. Lindsay was once again reminded why she could never move away from her hometown for good. Everyone looked out for each other here. People were concerned without being nosey. Well, sometimes they were a little nosey, but no harm was meant by it.

Lindsay peeked out the window next to the back door, gasped, and dropped to the floor before she could be spotted. An icy hand seemed to grasp her heart, undoing all the good that Harvey's help and invitation had done. It wasn't the plumber. It was someone whose arrival she'd been fearing and anticipating for months. It was Steve: her philandering, suspected arsonist, soon-to-be ex-husband.

Chapter Three

*In Which a Creepy Note Prompts
a Call to a Mischievous Elf*

Lindsay crawled through the kitchen. This couldn't be real. The only reasonable explanation she could come up with to account for Steve's presence outside her back door was that some awful fate had befallen him, and this was his ghost, returning to haunt her. Lindsay wouldn't object to the spirits of her Belgian ancestors popping by their old stomping grounds from time to time, but Steve? That was going too far. A husband who had a year long affair, tried to burn down her century old barn, and sneaked around her Halloween party in a gorilla suit didn't show up without warning for a friendly how-do-you-do. It just wasn't done. By the time Lindsay finally reached the living room, she was trembling. Grace was shifting furniture to make room for their tree.

"Why are you crawling?" Grace asked.

Oh, right. Lindsay stood. She clasped her hands

together so Grace wouldn't notice them shaking. It all came out in a rush. "Steve's here. He's here. Right now. He just appeared out of nowhere. What could he want? What do we do?"

"What do you mean he's here?" Grace looked behind her as if she expected him to stroll into the room and put up his feet in the easy chair.

"He's on the back steps. He just knocked at the door."

"You're kidding. I didn't hear anything. Is it locked?"

"No. I didn't want to lock it; he'd know I was right there. Besides, it wouldn't matter. He still has a key."

"Alright, let's get out of the window in case he comes around to the front door. He might've seen me already."

Lindsay didn't have to be told twice. She crouched against the wall next to the window the instant Grace suggested it. Grace joined her and they listened. The only sounds came from Harvey in the basement until Steve knocked for a second time. They waited for the click of the turning knob or the swoosh of the opening door, but neither materialized. The house creaked, the clock ticked, and the wind hissed in the chimney. Finally, the lights of Steve's truck swept through the room as he backed out of the driveway.

Lindsay poured out her breath in a long smooth stream. She and Grace stood up and peered outside. The yard was dark and quiet. Harvey's truck was parked on the side of the road. How had they missed it on their way home?

They crept into the kitchen. A note had been taped to the window. Grace flung open the door, grabbed the note, and scurried back inside.

"I can read it if you want me to," she said.

"I don't know if I can." Lindsay looked at the little yellow piece of paper warily, as if it might jump up at her and latch onto her face like an alien squid.

Grace opened the note, but Lindsay snatched it from her hand. Her mind raced. She couldn't imagine what Steve could possibly have to say to her after all this time, but she needed to be the one who read his message. She scanned through it twice, her hands trembling again, and crumpled it up. She walked over to the recycling bin and tossed it in. Grace plucked it back out.

"You should keep this. I can't imagine how you're feeling right now, and this has absolutely nothing to do with consideration for Steve, but if he ends up doing something crazy again, you're going to want a record of what happened."

Lindsay took it, holding on loosely, as if she wanted to fling it away or drop it on the floor and stomp it into oblivion. There was nothing menacing about the note, and that's what made it so uncomfortable to read. Steve made it sound as though they'd had a disagreement, mutually deciding to go their separate ways for a while.

Lindsay- I hope our time apart has

been as productive for you as it has been for me. I'd like to speak to you about everything that has happened between us in the last few months. I'll stop by again tomorrow afternoon so we can figure out where to go from here. We've both had a lot of time to think about what we want, and I'd like to explain a few things and make a request, if you'll give me the chance.

Steve

The fact that it wasn't a request wasn't lost on Lindsay. She handed the note to Grace, who scanned it quickly and made to throw it away herself. Lindsay stopped her. Grace had been right the first time. Steve was unbalanced, and there was no way of knowing what he might do next. Lindsay would keep the letter somewhere inconvenient, where she wouldn't be tempted to take it out and read it obsessively. The safe in her armoire would be the perfect spot. She'd put it there tonight when she went to bed. For now, she carried it into the kitchen and slid it under the silverware in one of the kitchen drawers. The two sisters sat down at the table.

"Well, what are we going to do now? He's coming back tomorrow afternoon," said Grace.

Lindsay had been wondering the same thing. It was comforting to think that her new guests should've arrived by then. She'd feel safer having witnesses. Steve was a charming person when he wanted to be, and he'd be on his best behavior if there were other people present. If he showed up and she asked him to leave when they were here alone, however, he would likely create a scene. She'd humor him, let him into the house and listen to what he had to say, then send him on his way. It sounded so simple, but she was kidding herself if she thought it was going to be that easy.

She told Grace her plan, and her sister looked concerned. "I have to work at the hospital all day tomorrow, remember? What if the guests don't stick around? I know they're going to be here at noon, but what if Steve shows up at two and our lodgers are already out playing Elmer Fudd? You'd be here alone with him."

"Good point. I could leave as well, but there's too much going on here for me to be hiding out somewhere all afternoon."

Grace brightened up. "You know who you should call? Grandma."

Lindsay waited for the punch line. When one didn't materialize, she asked, "Are you joking?"

"No. Think about it. You can't fight crazy, right? But maybe you can meet it head on with a different kind of crazy. She doesn't take nonsense, and I'm sorry, but she saw through Steve before anyone else did. Remember how she would drop hints about setting you up with someone else while you two were dating? Or when she pulled you aside before the wedding to remind you that you didn't have to tie yourself down yet?"

Lindsay remembered. At the time she thought it was just Grandma being Grandma, but she had to agree, she'd known that something about Lindsay's ill-fated romance wasn't right from the start.

"You can't kid a kidder," Lindsay said, echoing one of Grandma Vivian's famous lines.

"Let's call her right now."

"It's getting kind of late."

"Are you kidding? Grandma stays up later than we do."

Once again, Grace had a point. "Alright, I'll call her, but she might be busy tomorrow. You know how her social calendar fills up."

Lindsay made the call, half hoping she wouldn't reach her. The phone rang for a long time. Right before she was ready to hang up, her grandma answered, panting. "Lindsay? Sorry honey, I was doing a turbo dance aerobics class I found on-line. It's wild. I'll send you the link."

"Thanks. Sounds fun."

"Oh it is. I've got some new moves to try at the next senior shuffle. Those old folks won't know what hit 'em."

"I can't wait to check it out. I was calling because I'm wondering what you're up to tomorrow afternoon."

"Hmm...I was supposed to go cross country skiing with Esther, but she cancelled at the last minute. Let me take a look at my planner. I don't think I rescheduled that time slot." Paper shuffled in the background. "Nope. I'm free. Why? You want to go out on the town?"

"Not exactly. I have a group arriving tomorrow afternoon, and Steve is coming over too. I'd like to make sure someone else is here when I see him again."

"He is, is he? Is that something you asked him to do, or did he just inform you that he'd be showing his sorry face after all these months?"

"The showing his face one."

"Just as I thought. If that boy ever had a single good intention it would die of loneliness. I'll be there alright. I'll be there with an elf suit on. In fact, I'll stick around for a couple of nights. I just need to make some calls to clear my calendar."

"That's not necessary…"

She'd hung up.

"What did she say?" Grace asked.

Lindsay repeated her grandmother's words verbatim.

"Yes! Go Grandma," said Grace, pumping her fist. "I feel so much better now. Everything's going to be fine. Probably."

"Probably? This is going to be a disaster."

The whirlwind of energy and opinions that was their grandma added more uncertainty to an already precarious situation. Could Lindsay call her off, tell her it was a false alarm? Not a chance, aside from the guilt that would arise from lying to her grandma, it wouldn't work; in addition to numerous other talents developed over a lifetime of adventures, Grandma had uncanny lie detection skills.

"Do you really think she's going to show up in

an elf suit?" Grace asked.

"Yes. Don't you?"

"Absolutely. I wish I could be here. Take some pictures and send them to me."

"I'm glad someone finds this entertaining."

"Sorry. I shouldn't joke. I know it's going to be awful for you to see Steve again."

"It is, but it'll be a relief too. Now let's set up our tree," Lindsay said abruptly. She pulled Grace out of her chair, and they both bundled up and went outside. Their breath curved in frozen plumes as they carried the tree through the crunchy snow and up the stairs. Lindsay went into the basement to get the tree skirt and stand. Harvey was still there, stowing away his tools.

"Hey, I'm all finished," he said, rolling down the sleeves of his plaid shirt and hefting his bag over his shoulder. Flecks of orange paint covered his cheeks like freckles. He must've been out marking timber today. "Good thing you had that alarm."

"Yeah. We could've ended up with a swimming pool down here." As it was, everything was almost completely dry and clean already.

"Well, you shouldn't have trouble from that pipe any more."

Lindsay wanted to tell him again how much his help meant to her, but she couldn't bring herself to say it. Instead, she said, "Have a good night. I'll see you Sunday."

"See you," he said, heading up the stairs. He called goodbye to Grace and went out the door. Lindsay ran upstairs and turned the deadbolt behind him.

She and Grace set up the tree and strung it with lights. Grace grabbed the box of ornaments, which was filled to the brim with family heirlooms. Lindsay pulled out a little blown glass airplane.

"Remember this one?" she asked.

"Of course. Grandma got it for me when I went to Germany for that semester abroad. You never came to visit me. It would've been so much fun. You still haven't flown anywhere, have you?"

Lindsay shook her head and pulled out another ornament. The thought of zooming along in a metal tube thousands of feet in the air terrified her. It didn't seem like it should work.

"What about this one?" asked Lindsay. It was a just married ornament that her parents had gotten for their first Christmas together. Two lovebirds kissed in the center of a porcelain heart. They hadn't taken any of their ornaments to Florida, not being the sentimental types.

"Or this one," said Grace, pulling out a horse figurine. "Grandma made it for you, didn't she? Remember how much you loved our horses as a kid? When did you decide not to have them anymore?"

"It's been quite a few years..." Lindsay trailed off. She couldn't remember deciding not to get another one when her two lovely old mares passed away. Steve had never cared for them, claiming they took up too much of her time. Now that he was gone, that was very true. It would've been too much for her to care for them on top of everything else. Their beautiful old sleigh sat idle in the barn now. It had been a lovely sight when the horses pulled it through the snowy fields.

The tree filled up quickly with Santas, snow-men, reindeer, and colorful glass shapes of all kinds.

"What about your new ornament?" Grace asked.

"I can't believe I almost forgot it." Lindsay went into the kitchen and opened the box. Something stuck out amongst the folds of tissue. It was a note she hadn't spotted earlier. *Merry Christmas to a brave and beautiful woman. Love, Your secret admirer.*

How sweet. Sticking it in her pocket, Lindsay went back into the living room with her ornament; Grace was sitting on the couch, admiring the tree. Lindsay hung the ornament front and center. Who could have written that message? It meant more to her than its sender would ever know. She hoped she'd get a chance to tell them. Would they reveal them-selves? It could be one of her friends or-and she knew she shouldn't even be considering this, because of the obvious complications it would cause-it could be Harvey.

Wait a minute, speaking of complications, what if it was Steve? She'd considered it before, but the tone of the note was totally inappropriate. Then again, she hadn't expected him to show up out of the blue, either. He was brazen, but surely sending her love notes would be going too far. He wouldn't dare to try to win her back after everything that had happened. Or would he? She'd find out tomorrow, whether she wanted to or not.

Chapter Four

In Which Grandma Decks the Halls

The next morning, Lindsay awoke to the smell of pancakes browning on the stove. She stretched and looked at the clock. That couldn't be right. Was it really 8:00 already? Grace would've left for work by now. Had she made pancakes before she left? It smelled like coffee too. How thoughtful of her.

Lindsay jumped out of bed and skipped down the stairs. She should've been up hours ago. She bounded into the kitchen, ready to grab a pancake from the fridge, but was stopped in her tracks by the sight of her grandma flipping them in-they'd guessed it-an elf suit.

"Grandma?"

"Don't look so surprised. I said I'd be here, didn't I? Now pop a squat and I'll bring you a coffee. I made fruit salad too. That flibbertigibbet of a sister of yours left an hour ago. She says she'll be thinking of you today, for all the good that'll do ya."

She tossed a blueberry pancake into the air for emphasis. It flew over her shoulder and landed on the floor. Grandma picked it up, blew it off, and threw it back in the pan. Lindsay sat down meekly, making a mental note of which pancake to avoid. There was no arguing with Grandma Vivian.

"Alright, let's discuss the game plan," the elf chef said.

"I haven't really…"

"Of course you haven't. That's what I'm here for. Let's see. Grace told me your next group should be arriving at noon. That gives us a little less than four hours to whip this place into shape."

Lindsay took a sip of coffee. She thought it looked pretty good around here. They had been planning on having a guest yesterday as well after all, but she'd play along. It might be nice to have someone else in charge for a day.

"Did that man, whose name I will not mention, say what time he would be making his big appearance?" Grandma asked.

"The note said he'd be here sometime in the afternoon."

Her grandma snorted and plopped two pancakes onto a plate, setting them in front of her. Shoot. Lindsay had forgotten to keep her eye on the floor one.

"We'd better get rocking then," Grandma said. "I'm going to need you to get dressed in something fabulous. If you have an elf suit as well, so much the better, but either way you're going to want to make an impression. Don't you dare go up there and throw on a pair of jeans and a fleece. I'm not having anyone thinking a granddaughter of mine can be played around with like a marionette."

Her grandmother's outfit certainly did make an impression. Red and white striped stockings stuck out beneath a ruffled skirt. A green blouse, cinched with a black belt, was studded with red and gold buttons. All that was missing was the pointy hat. Wait, scratch that. The hat was on the counter next to the fridge. It was topped with a golden bell.

Should Lindsay ask why the elf suit was so essential to this operation? No, it was Grandma Logic, which defied regular logic. She'd never been able to wrap her mind around her methods, but Grandma always ended up on top, so she must have had something figured out that Lindsay hadn't been able to grasp yet.

While they ate, Lindsay went over everything that had happened the day before. When she mentioned the gift that had been left on the back landing, her grandma pushed away from the table. "I almost forgot; this was outside when I got here. You must have quite the admirer." She handed Lindsay another box. The green and red plaid wrapping paper was familiar, but this gift was larger than the one from yesterday.

Lindsay lifted the tag. Once again, her name was written across it. Inside was a fluffy white hand-knitted scarf. Exquisitely soft, it was crafted into a beautiful cable pattern. She wrapped it around her neck and checked for another note. There was one, folded into the tissue paper once again. *Cozy Christmas Wishes. Love, Your secret admirer.*

Her grandma read over her shoulder. "Ha! This is perfect. You can tell Steve that you've already picked up a new beau."

Lindsay handed Grandma the scarf so she could feel its cottony softness. "It's most likely from one of my friends."

Her grandma rubbed the scarf between her fingers before handing it back "Friends, schmends. You don't realize the effect you have on men. Look at you. You and Grace got your looks from my side of the family, you know."

Lindsay looked down. She wore comfy striped flannel pajamas and fuzzy purple socks. Not exactly the picture of glamour, but she'd take the compliment. "You were making suggestions about what we can do to get ready for Steve," she reminded Grandma.

"Right. I'll take over down here. You go upstairs and get yourself ready. It looks like the rooms are in order, but I'm going to make some little changes." Grandma wiggled her fingers and waved them around. What, exactly, was she going to do?

"Alright, off I go," said Lindsay.

She headed to her room, tempted to sneak back down to see what kind of magic the octogenarian elf was planning, but changed her mind. Like so many things in life, it would be more fun if it was a surprise. Besides, there was a good chance that she wouldn't like what she saw, and she wanted to trust the process.

When Lindsay came back downstairs an hour later, hoping her look would be up to par, she nearly staggered back at the changes that had been wrought, and she hadn't gone beyond the kitchen yet. Sprigs of mistletoe hung in every door frame. Red, green, and gold pompons were draped above the window. A kitchen Christmas tree with molasses cookie ornaments stood in the corner, topped with a Santa oven mitt. Festive utensils filled the kitchen canister to the brim. Snowflake plates and a pine branch centerpiece sat atop a holiday table runner.

Lindsay strode into the living room, where there was-no surprise here-more mistletoe. In addition to the door frame, mistletoe hung above the fireplace, the tree, and the couch. A fire was crackling. The couch was so laden with holiday throw pillows that a spot to sit would prove elusive without some major rearranging. Nutcrackers had been added to the hearth, and a garland graced the mantle.

Another garland adorned the painting over the couch. Lindsay made some strategic adjustments to the glittery strand to reveal three women lounging at a picnic table amongst a bucolic scene. Grandma folded a holiday quilt then draped it over the reading chair. A red feather boa twisted around her neck.

"What do you think?" asked Grandma Viv, spreading her arms wide and twirling around.

"I think an elf did quite a number on our house. It's beautiful."

"Why thank you. You look lovely, yourself."

Lindsay donned a sparkly v-neck sweater that brought out the green in her hazel eyes. "Don't you want to take a rest?" she asked. "I can't believe you did all of this in an hour. Where'd you get the tree?"

Grandma shrugged and Lindsay made a mental note to check if there were any blank spaces in the spruce screen on the far side of the summer kitchen.

"You didn't say anything about my fabulous boa," Grandma said, twirling it with one hand.

"It's great. It really ties your outfit together."

"Thank you. It also doubles as a lasso, in case any husbands try to bolt before they've explained themselves." She whipped it around her head and tossed one end towards the couch.

Lindsay was speechless, but also grateful. Grandma knew what she was doing. Instead of worrying and breaking into cold sweats, Lindsay had spent the morning keeping up with her antics.

Lindsay went into the kitchen and started mixing up bread for the day. Grandma continued to scoot in and out of the house, her arms full of decorations.

By noon, the house was declared ready. At five after, a wrapping at the front door produced a sturdy man in his early seventies. He smiled at Lindsay, revealing a large gap between his front teeth, and took off his sunglasses. His close cropped hair and beard were a matching salt and pepper gray.

Shaking Lindsay's hand with a shockingly strong grip, he boomed, "Brian Wilkerson, at your service. I'm thrilled to be here, just thrilled. Gotta go where the action is, am I right?"

"We're thrilled to have you," said Lindsay, joggling her hand to bring the feeling back to her fingertips. If he was looking for action, she wasn't sure he had come to the right place. "Come on in."

He stomped the snow off his boots and stepped inside. "Thank you. I've got two men in my crew. They should be here in a couple hours."

His crew? Something about him-his look and demeanor-conjured up images of a gung-ho Englishman on safari. He even had a khaki jacket. All he lacked was the pith helmet and monocle.

Lindsay led him to his room. He gazed out the window. As requested, his accommodations faced directly over the orchard. "This view is ideal. I have some equipment to carry in. I'll be right back."

Ideal for what? He stomped back down the stairs before Lindsay could inquire. She returned to the kitchen and pulled out a loaf of bread. Her new guest passed in and out of the house with bulging duffle bags and some kind of strange binoculars. Was that a gun case? What was going on around here? Between the crazy decorations and the arrival of Colonel Mustard, Lindsay struggled to convince herself she wasn't dreaming. Just wait until her grandma spotted him. He was exactly her type: handsome, years younger, and almost as loud as she was.

Right on cue, the vivacious matriarch joined her at the stove. "So, what's the new lodger like? I heard him from the living room. He sounds like a nice hearty young lad."

"He's not all that young..."

"Why, hello there." Her grandma struck a pose, one knee bent and hands on hips, as Brian came back through the kitchen with another duffle bag. What on earth was he up to?

Meeting her at the stove, Brian took her grandma's hand and kissed it. "Lindsay didn't mention she had a sister," he said.

"She wishes. I'm her mother, Vivian. So pleased to make your acquaintance."

"The pleasure is all mine, I assure you."

Mother? It was time for Lindsay to break this up. "Lunch will be ready whenever you are."

"Excellent. I've worked up a hearty appetite." Brian patted his khaki stomach. "I'm just going to drop off the last of my things and I'll be down. We have so much to talk about."

"Sounds great." This wasn't a dream. It was worse. This was a bizarre theatrical production, and Lindsay had shown up in the middle without a script. She'd just have to improvise.

When Brian had gone upstairs, Vivian pulled off the tree topper mitt and used it as a makeshift fan. "What a man."

"Alright, Grandma. Simmer down. He's our guest. Remember my rule about guests?"

"Vaguely."

"Hands off."

"Meh."

"No. Not meh. Steer clear."

"Yeah, yeah. Shh...here he comes." She popped the mitt back onto the tree.

Brian sat down at the table. He took a big bite of his sandwich. "Delicious. Just delicious. I assume you know why I'm here."

He said this in the direction of both women, and Lindsay wondered for a moment if her grandma had some inkling. How could she though? She had only agreed to come over last night.

When neither woman answered, Brian turned to face them, draping his arm around the back of his chair. "The Sasquatch, of course, I'm hunting the Sasquatch. I was scouring the mountains of Oregon when a rumor reached me about a sighting that happened on Halloween in a tiny village called Namur. Well, I had to look it up, had never heard of it of course. Imagine my surprise when I saw that it was right at the base of a peninsula that looked like a little Wisconsin thumb's up. I took it as a sign and rushed over here as quick as I could."

Ah yes, the Sasquatch. Lindsay knew exactly what he was referring to. She was personally acquainted with this particular Sasquatch. Unbeknownst to her, Steve had shown up at her Halloween party in a gorilla costume. When he was discovered by Chloe, she trapped him in a porta potty and dragged it down the road with a truck until she reached the home of the local newspaper reporter. When the reporter let him out, Steve fled into the woods before his identity could be ascertained.

As often happens in small towns, rumors flew, and the tale was passed along until boring old Steve had been transformed into a shaggy Sasquatch who had dragged a porta potty down the road with his own massive strength and was planning to live in it. How he locked himself in from the outside was a complication that didn't quite fit the story, so it was ignored in favor of the idea that the reporter was part of some kind of government cover-up. The story was all very complicated, ridiculous, and therefore heartily endorsed as truth by most who heard it.

Unfortunately, Lindsay couldn't tell this eager man that his quarry was really a scoundrel in a Halloween costume. She was sworn to secrecy.

"Yes. I've heard those rumors too, but I haven't seen a Sasquatch here at all," she said.

Brian nodded. "I was told you'd say that."

"By whom?"

"I can't reveal my sources. Suffice to say there's a vast network of cryptozoologists such as myself, and stealth and subterfuge is a key part of our success."

Lindsay leaned against the counter. Brian wasn't exactly stealthy about his mission. She decided right then and there to humor him, though. This may be exactly the kind of outlandish distraction she needed to stay sane during her first Christmas alone. "I understand. I'll use my utmost discretion."

"Excellent. I knew I could count on you. It's your face. You have that hearty Midwestern look."

"Thank you?"

"You say you haven't seen the creature, but my sources inform me that he was found in a portable toilet that was rented by you for a Halloween party."

"That's true. I hold events in my barn. The porta potty disappeared during the party, and returned just as mysteriously at the end of the night."

Brian stroked his beard. "You don't say...and that's the extent of your knowledge?"

"I'm afraid so."

"It's all making sense. The Sasquatch could've easily slipped by your guests. He would've blended in of course, because of the costumes."

"That does make a lot of sense," said Lindsay.

The entire time this exchange was going on, Grandma Vivian had been looking from one to the other of them like she was watching a tennis match. She appeared to be alternating between deciding these two were crazy or joining in on the madness on the off chance that it would bring her closer to the rugged Bigfoot hunter.

Evidently she made up her mind to join in, because she said, "I've lived here for most of my life, and I can tell you that there's something mysterious going on. You should stick around and search high and low. I'd be happy to act as your local guide."

Lindsay was onto her ruse, but Brian was enthralled. He pulled out a chair and invited Vivian to join him. Lindsay, not interested in staying to listen to her grandma's fabrications, made an excuse to take her leave.

"I need to head outside," she said.

They didn't hear her. Vivian was already embellishing tales of a mysterious shaggy creature that stalked the woods of her childhood. Lindsay went outside and sat down on the porch. She pulled out her phone. There was a message from Chloe: *Talked to Bea and Sarah. Betsy and Grace are in!*

Lindsay replied: *Yay!*

This coming year, despite all of its uncertainty, would be a good one for the Demeter Society. In addition to adding two new members, they had big plans: several conferences to attend, more farming workshops for women, and a fundraising carnival. Lindsay never could've imagined that Grace would be back, helping out with the inn and now possibly joining her society for women in farming, but now that she was here, Lindsay wouldn't have it any other way.

After pocketing her phone, she picked up a shovel and scraped bits of ice off the back steps. Brian had pulled his truck up close to the barn. Two Bigfoot silhouettes were stuck to his back window. The attached trailer had been painted with a wooded scene. A Sasquatch loomed in the foreground. Lindsay was so intently curious about her new guest's obsession that she didn't notice a familiar truck pulling into her driveway until it was too late to head for cover.

Chapter Five

In Which a Man Who Deserves Coal Asks for Something More

L indsay looked up just in time to see Steve standing beside the Bigfoot trailer with a beard he'd never sported before and a jacket and boots she didn't recognize.

The last time she'd seen him, they had just climbed into bed on a warm summer's night. The windows were open. She had taken a shower and pulled on her pretty blue nightgown, hoping he would notice but not really expecting him to. He was reading a book, some Scandinavian thriller, and didn't look over as she slid next to him and wrapped her arm around his stomach. He kissed her forehead and went back to reading. She kissed his cheek. No response. After a while, Lindsay rolled over on her side facing away from her husband. She fell asleep to the sound of flipping pages.

The following morning, Lindsay awoke early.

Something felt different. Steve's side of the bed was neatly made. Lindsay sat up. A note was folded in half, tented on the bulge that his pillow made under the quilt. It informed her that he had left and may never return.

Lindsay checked the armoire, where most of his clothes and his suitcase had disappeared. His toothbrush and razor were missing from the bathroom as well. The emptiness that had threatened to engulf her on that morning in mid summer had been retreating, however slowly, over the fall and early winter. It folded back over her now.

"Hey there. You're looking great," Steve said, as if they were acquaintances who hadn't seen each other in a while.

Lindsay had so many questions queuing in the back of her throat that no single one could get through. Where had be been? Why did he leave? How dare he show up here as if nothing had happened? She looked down at her hands, willing herself not to let him see her cry. Finally, she said, "I'd be more comfortable if we talked inside."

He nodded and followed her up the stairs and into the kitchen.

"Well look who the cat dragged in," Grandma said, standing up with her hands firmly on her hips. She wasn't trying to look seductive this time. This was her "don't mess with me" look.

Brian didn't look up from the map spread before him. Lindsay made her way straight through the kitchen and so did Steve, who must've known better than to say a single word to the grandmother of the woman he had jilted.

"That's right, keep walking," Grandma said under her breath but loud enough to be clearly audible. She called louder next. "Lindsay, holler if you need me. I'm trained in jujitsu, in case anyone was wondering."

When they got to the living room, Lindsay stood with her arms crossed and faced Steve, waiting for him to speak first. He sat on the couch and gulped, lowering his head.

"How have you been?" he said quietly to his knees. They didn't respond and neither did Lindsay, not at first anyway.

Her throat was burning. Finally, she choked out a response. "I'm figuring out how to make things work around here."

"I see that. Good for you."

At those words, a rush of adrenaline coursed through her and anger began to override her sadness. "Good for me? What about you? What are you doing here? What do you want from me? You disappear with no warning. You try to burn down my barn…"

He held up his hands, defending himself against the accusations that she hurled his way. "I didn't do that; I didn't try to burn down the barn."

"Who did then? Your truck was parked outside when the fire started."

He looked up. "I was coming to see you, but then I changed my mind and left. That's all. I don't know anything about it beyond that."

"Coming to see me? At one in the morning? Please." She scoffed.

"I was on my way to visit my cousin in Boise. My flight left at some ridiculous hour, and I passed your house on my way. I was thinking about you and hoping maybe you'd be awake...that we could talk...I don't know. I've been really conflicted."

Lindsay looked him the eye. "You happened to stop by when an electrical fire started in the barn and then you left the state for a month? If someone hadn't been driving past, it would be nothing but a pile of ashes now."

"I know. The police questioned me though, and everything I'm saying to you checks out. There may have been something else going on, but it wasn't me." He gazed up at her beseechingly, and there was some part of her that wanted to believe him, but there was so much more that had happened since then that it really wouldn't matter if he was telling the truth about the fire.

"What about..." She couldn't finish her sentence, but she didn't have to.

"Yes. I admit it. I was seeing someone else. It was a big mistake. I didn't mean for it to happen."

He didn't mean for it to happen? Please. Things like that didn't just happen. At some point, a choice was made that led to a whole bunch of other choices that he'd never be able to take back. Lindsay had heard enough.

"Please tell me why you're here so we can get this over with. I've been completely in the dark for months, and I want to get everything in order so I can move on."

He cleared his throat. "I know I don't have a right to ask for anything from you."

"No. You don't."

"But I'm making one last request."

Skepticism and impatience radiated from her and he hesitated. "Go ahead," she said. Whatever it took for this to be over was going to be fine by her. She'd been through much worse.

"I'd like you to give me one more chance."

What? She hadn't expected that. There was absolutely no way she was giving him a second chance, no way that she could ever trust him enough to let him back into her heart again. Her answer was a simple, "No."

"Just hear me out. Please. I made a huge mistake. I didn't realize what we had together until it was gone. There's no one else in the world like you."

Lindsay started to speak, but Steve interrupted her. "I don't expect you to take me back right now, but I'd like to come by sometimes, just to help out with things around the house. I'll stay out of your way. You don't even have to talk to me if you don't want to. I want to prove to you that you can count on me. I'll wait for as long as it takes, even if that means waiting for the rest of my life."

She was unmoved. "I'm sorry, but I really can't imagine a scenario in which I can trust you again. I want a divorce."

His eyes spilled over with tears. "I understand

that you feel that way right now, but let's give it a little more time. I know it doesn't seem like it, but the vows I made to you mean something to me."

Who was he kidding?

"I wasn't myself for a while, but living without you has made me realize that I don't want to lose you ever again." He put his head in his hands and sobbed.

Lindsay had never seen him cry before, and there was a small part of her that was moved. She had been happy with her husband for the vast majority of their seven years of marriage. Hadn't she? She thought so, but now she wasn't so sure. She thought he'd been happy too, and look how that had turned out. On the other hand, they shared so much history: inside jokes, struggles, triumphs, quirks, everything. They'd been a team, until they weren't anymore. A shred of sympathy struggled under the weight of weeks and months of painful uncertainty and the sting of betrayal.

"I need some time to think," she said. Although every instinct she possessed was screaming at her to boot him out the door and slam it behind him, she didn't want to make a rash decision that she might one day regret. She wasn't committing to anything; she could change her mind the second he left, but it couldn't hurt to talk to Grace tonight and get her perspective.

"Thank you," he said. "Just consider it. That's all I ask. I would do anything to make this up to you." He rubbed the moisture from beneath his red eyes and stood to leave. "This is going to sound a little weird, but can I get a picture of you and Grandma? I don't have a single picture of the two of you together. I know she's not happy with me right now, but I never knew my grandparents, and she looks so...so memorable in that elf suit."

Not happy was an understatement, so was memorable. "You can ask her yourself," Lindsay finally said.

"Thank you. You stay here. I'll get her." Steve left and came back with a scowling elf.

"Let's get this over with. Where do you want me?" Grandma asked.

"Could we get one of you two on the couch?"

Lindsay and Grandma sat side by side and smiled as Steve took their picture. "Thank you. I'm going to be totally alone on Christmas this year. This photo means a lot to me."

"Uh huh," said Grandma. "See you." She headed back into the kitchen.

Lindsay stood as well. She and Steve faced each other in the living room. His eyelids drooped. He gave her a weak grin. "I don't know how I'll ever forgive myself if we don't make it through this. You're just..." he shook his head, at a loss for words. "This place is the best home I've ever known." He walked out of the room and Lindsay followed behind him.

Entering the kitchen, Lindsay and Steve were met with the sight of Grandma and Brian, poring over a map of Namur.

"Here's where the old hermit lived. Right here on our property, and..." Grandma looked up at Steve.

"Oh. You're still here. You got your picture, and you better have been giving a whole bunch of apologies while you two were talking in there. Now scoot, off you go."

Grandma ushered him out the door, slammed it so hard some dust fell from the frame, and sat back down to carry on with her tale. Before she did, though, she turned to Lindsay and said, "I heard the whole thing. You did well. Told him what's what."

Lindsay could've acted horrified, but she'd spied the tell-tale end of a feather boa fluttering at the edge of the living room door frame. It magically disappeared the second Steve suggested going to find Grandma.

"I'm not going to tell you what to do," Vivian continued, "but don't you dare let him back. If his brains were leather, he wouldn't have enough to saddle a June bug. I was married to your grandpa...I mean father, for...let's just say many years, and Steve isn't fit to shine his shoes. You deserve so much better."

"I don't know..." said Lindsay.

"Look, I get it. Taking relationship advice from me is like getting construction tips from the three little pigs. One notable success and I think I'm an expert."

"It's not that, Grandma. I appreciate your help and your advice, but I need some time to think. This is a big decision. I need to make it on my own."

"I know you do. Didn't I say right away I'm not going to tell you what to do?"

Lindsay sighed. "I'll be in my room for a bit."

She was ready to apologize to Brian. This whole scene was incredibly unprofessional, but either he didn't notice that anything was going on around him, or he didn't care, because once again he didn't look up. Instead, he muttered to himself and scribbled notes in a thick black ledger.

"Right here, you say?" he asked Grandma, pointing at the map. "What year would that have been?"

Lindsay went upstairs and climbed into bed. For a long time after Steve left this summer, she slept on her side of the bed, just as she had throughout their marriage. Then one morning she woke up sprawled across the middle. She never went back after that.

What was she going to do? She did miss her husband, the husband that she thought she had. This new person, the man who sat in her living room and begged her to let him back into her life, was a stranger to her. He had killed and buried the man she thought he was, and there was no way to revive him. She knew this to be true, so why was she tempted, even slightly, to give Steve another chance?

Chapter Six

In Which All Three Wise(ish) Men Convene at the Inn

L indsay awoke to the sound of slamming doors and yelling. How long had she been asleep? The clock offered reassuring news this time. Only ten minutes had passed. She gave herself a look in the mirror, smoothed out her sweater and hair, and bounded into the kitchen. Grandma and Brian were still at the table, heads scandalously close together, making notes and formulating a plan of action.

Lindsay slipped past them and went outside. Two burly men were unloading a conversion van. From the neck down, they wore shaggy camouflage suits, making them look more like piles of seaweed than country house lodgers. From the neck up, their bushy beards and camo hats didn't provide much contrast with their outfits.

With any luck, someone would mistake them for swamp creatures, and Lindsay would never have a shortage of business again. The only question was if these were the types of customers she wanted to attract. She had no objection to eccentric characters-there were more than a few in her own family-but in terms of the amount of rope she had left, she felt she had just about reached the end, and these two didn't look like the sorts whose stay would be uncompli-cated. In other words, Lindsay could handle some ex-citement on occasion, but this was all becoming a bit much.

What Lindsay had mistaken for shouting turned out to be the normal volume level of these men's conversations.

"Hook, did you grab the sardines? We need to get 'em into the freezer."

"They're right here. You think I want my truck to smell like a chum bucket again?"

"More than it already does?"

"Bah." Hook swung the pail at his buddy and rancid liquid sloshed out. Lindsay could smell it from there. They weren't thinking of bringing that stuff in-side, were they?

They headed for the front door with their bags and the dripping bucket of sludge. Lindsay called them over before they could slosh fish juice onto her front porch.

"Hello? You can come in the back door."

They turned around and strode up the drive-way, their muddy boots leaving massive footprints in the snow.

"Hi there! I'm Captain Hook, but you can just

call me Hook. You must be Lindsay. I see Brian's here already. He hasn't been giving you any trouble has he?"

When Hook arrived at the steps, he set down his bucket and bags. He reached out to shake Lindsay's hand and she took it, careful not to touch her clothes afterwards.

"He's in the kitchen," she said. "It sounds like you three are on quite a mission."

"I'd say," the other man came up and set his load down as well. "We're in for a million dollar reward if we can provide evidence that leads to the capture of Bigfoot. I'm Moose, by the way." He shook her hand as well.

"Come on in. Do you need help with anything?" Lindsay asked, hoping they wouldn't ask her to carry the bucket.

"Nah. We're used to lugging this business around," said Hook.

They followed Lindsay inside. She winced as they plopped everything down on her beautiful wood floor. Drips of rancid water pooled at the base of the bucket. She needed to say something. That rotten fish smell might never come out if she didn't act fast.

"Do you need somewhere to put your bucket? I have a shed out back that might work."

"Nah," said Moose. "The thing about that is, Sasquatch have a sense of smell that's about a thousand times better than ours, and they love sardines more than anything. I can't tell you how many times we've left the bait in a garage and ended up losing the lot of them. They're sneaky about it too, using other animals to do their work for them."

Lindsay nodded. Apparently listening to outlandish claims was the rule of the day today, and she found that the more she heard, the better she was at keeping her face pencil straight. "I can see how that would happen, yes. I'm afraid it won't fit in my freezer though. We could put it in the summer kitchen and lock the door. It's quite secure."

Both men followed Lindsay back outside. During the entire exchange, their leader hadn't looked up or acknowledged their arrival in any way. Brian marked up his map and grilled Vivian on the finer points of her story. Lindsay was almost impressed at how creative her grandmother could be. Almost, but not entirely, having experienced her ability to fabricate stories on the spot too many times to be fully impressed by this particular tall tale.

When Lindsay and the two newcomers reached the summer kitchen, the men circled it to check its air-tightness. A squat stone shed, the kitchen had been used by generations of women in Lindsay's family during the sweltering months of summer. A brick oven attached to the back of the building allowed them to bake their bread and pies without heating up the already uncomfortably hot house.

Apparently finding it satisfactory, the men nodded, so Lindsay slipped the padlock off and pulled open the rough wooden door. It was never actually locked. Unlike the house, there was nothing in here that would be of interest to a potential thief. The aromatic bucket was left on the ground, and Lindsay made a show of clicking the lock shut before leading the men back inside.

Hook and Moose pulled off their boots and tossed them on the mat. They flipped around two kitchen chairs and straddled them before taking in their surroundings. Unlike the rest of the house, which Lindsay had restored as close as possible to its original Belgian farmhouse aesthetic, the kitchen was modern, with a stainless convection oven and commercial stove.

"This is quite the fancy digs you have here," said Moose.

"Thank you," said Lindsay. "It's been in my family since the 1880s. We've had the land for twenty years longer than that, but the original log house was lost in the Peshtigo Fire."

Moose whistled. "Our accommodations are usually a lot more rustic. We're living out of tents half the time. That's alright in the Pacific Northwest, but I've never felt cold like a Midwest cold."

Hook agreed. "Our last stop was an old fleabag motel in North Dakota. They don't have snow there yet, but the wind whipped across those plains like a banshee." He scratched his head and Lindsay prayed that he didn't literally have fleas.

"Fill us in on what's going on here, old man." Moose slapped his hand on the map, making Lindsay jump.

Brian looked up for the first time, as if just noticing the presence of his two giant yelling comrades in camo. "We've hit a goldmine here, boys. The incident on Halloween is just the beginning. There have been sightings going back to the late 1940s at least. How this got past us, I have no idea. Apparently it's been a closely guarded secret."

Both men looked like Christmas had come early. "Get outta here. Says who?"

"Says her," said Brian, jerking a thumb at Vivian, who greeted both men with a smile.

"Why are you sharing this now?" Hook asked with a trace of skepticism.

"Nobody worth telling ever asked," Vivian replied. "But you three, I can tell you're the genuine article."

"So, what's the story?"

Brian repeated the outlandish tale. It started with a hermit, known only to some curious children and a select few farmers. That part of the story was true. His name was Hiram, and he had lived alone in the back woods on their property until his death sometime in the 1980s, just before Lindsay was born.

Her great-grandfather had fought in the war with him, and when they returned, one of the men started a family and carried on with his life, in a fashion, while the other faced struggles that he never fully overcame. Hiram built a shack out back and survived by hardscrabble determination and the kindness of locals.

From that verifiable foundation, a fantastical tale unfolded of a haunted loner who befriended a huge simian creature. The creature never knowingly revealed himself to anyone else, but a few intrepid children and rugged old-timers caught fleeting glimpses of him from afar. It was a compelling tale. Lindsay had never heard a word of it until now.

"This is it, boys. Vivian here has seen the creature herself, with her own eyes," said Brian.

"Have you ever seen a Sasquatch?" Lindsay asked the men, pouring coffees and passing them around. She set a tray of appetizers on the table and the hunters devoured them three at a time.

"We've discovered plenty of evidence," said Brian, "footprints, hair, blood, vocalizations, but they're too wily to allow themselves to be seen. They've evolved to avoid us and our cameras, and they're nocturnal. I don't need to prove anything to anyone though."

"No, of course not. I was just curious. I've never met Bigfoot hunters before. This is all new to me. So I take it a sighting is rare?"

"Extremely. People come to us with accounts of seeing them all the time, but 99% of them are either making it up or have let their imaginations run wild."

"So how do you know when someone's telling the truth?"

Brian looked thoughtful. "Well, a lot of the guys who've seen them seem almost angry about it. That'd be your loggers, ranchers, people like that. They consider themselves to be the toughest guys out there and they're not pleased about being intimidated by anything. Those guys I tend to believe.

Then there are people like your mother here, who've never told their story to anyone. The way I see it, if you were going to make something like that up, you wouldn't have waited forty years to do it."

Try seventy, Lindsay thought.

"That's right," Lindsay's "mother" said. "I was only a girl, and it only happened once. My parents had forbidden me to go into that part of the woods or have anything to do with the man who lived there. There were rumors about that area of the forest, about strange sounds coming from the hermit's cabin late at night.

"Of course, the fact that it was forbidden made it all the more fascinating to me. I used to sneak over there sometimes and visit with Hiram. He appeared ancient to me then, but he couldn't have been much past thirty. Living outdoors had aged him, and I don't think the flask he kept in his pocket was doing him any favors either. His skin was rough and weathered and he had a strange way about him, sometimes friendly and talkative, other times unpredictable and full of rage.

"While playing tag with friends in the orchard one fall evening, I found myself alone at the edge of the forest. I got it into my head to check on Hiram. It had been getting chilly, and I was worried about him. My mother brought him soup and blankets, but his shack was tumbledown and spare. I crept through the woods, trying to be quiet in case he was in a bad way. When I was nearly there, a shaggy man-he looked massive to me, must've been seven feet tall-lurched out from behind a clump of bushes and ran away into the forest, vanishing as mysteriously as he'd come. I ran home faster than poop through a goose (pardon my French) and didn't return to that part of the woods for months. That was the only time I saw it. I wonder now…"

"Yes?" All three men said. They hadn't taken their eyes from her during the entire tale.

"Well, that man, he was out there all alone. As a child, I wanted to help him, and I wonder if that creature didn't feel the same. There couldn't be very many of them, of those Bigfeet. Maybe he was alone too. Maybe they looked out for each other somehow."

Lindsay went to the sink and started washing dishes. How much of this story was pure invention? Her grandma sounded as though she had convinced herself that it was true.

Lindsay had heard stories about Hiram, and the little she knew about her great-grandfather led her to wonder if he had truly fared much better. He had managed to keep the farm going and raise a family, but she remembered him as a quiet, fidgety man with an air of sadness about him. Her grandma's brother had seemed incredibly protective of his father, and had become the man of the house at an early age.

"You said there have been more sightings?" Brian confirmed.

"I did say that. Didn't I?" Grandma said. "Yes. There have been rumors…you'll have to ask around. And he showed up at Halloween, of course…" Her eyes lit up. "Oh yes, ask Janine Martel at Martel's Grocery.

She's been aware of an unusual presence in this town for ages." She jabbed at the map and Brian circled the grocery store.

"What do you think, men?" Brian asked. "I would suggest we head out to the woods, but it's getting dark. My preference would be to do reconnaissance in the vicinity of the hermit's shed tomorrow morning, if that's alright with you."

Lindsay nodded. "I don't mind at all. As far as I know, it's still standing, but it may be difficult to find in the snow. This summer it was surrounded by saplings and covered with vines. It's little more than a frame covered with a rotten roof."

"Right. We'll scour the area. Vivian here has given us a fairly clear idea as to its location. As I was saying, the forest is out for tonight, but we could head over to the grocery store."

Grandma looked ready to let someone else take over with the storytelling for a while. She couldn't resist being in on the action, though. "I'll come with you tomorrow, if you'll have me," she said.

Brian clapped his hands together and beamed. "Fantastic." He turned to Lindsay. "What about you?"

"What about me?"

"I think it would be helpful if you came along. The Sasquatch had singled out your home for a reason. You may be a key player in this operation."

Lindsay raised her hands in protest. "I promise you, I'm just an ordinary person who is not the key to anything."

"Nonsense," Grandma Vivian chimed in. "She

has a very unusual aura, has since she was a kid."

"Excellent. Do you have ghillie suits?"

The two women looked at each other. Lindsay thought it sounded like something from Harry Potter perhaps.

Hook helped them out. "They're these get-ups we're wearing. These won't do us any good out here. We're going to need our snow ghillies tomorrow. We've got extras, if you don't have any on hand."

"Perfect. We're in," said Grandma. She gave Lindsay a pleading look.

"We're in," Lindsay agreed half-heartedly. It would make her Grandma's day if they were in on this together.

"Alright," said Brian, pushing away from the table and gathering up his map and notebook. "We'll keep you up to date on any developments after we've completed more interviews."

The men clomped out the door. When they had driven away, Lindsay asked her Grandma, "Be honest. Did you really see something in the woods?"

"I really did. Cross my heart." Grandma grabbed a washcloth and wiped down the table while Lindsay dried the coffee mugs and put them in the cupboard.

"Why didn't you ever tell me?" Lindsay asked.

"What would you have thought if I had?"

"That you were making things up."

"Exactly. That's why I never told anyone at all. I wasn't even supposed to be out there. I can't say for sure what I saw. Maybe it was a bear, or maybe I was pretending or had a dream and filled in the details. You know how childhood memories can be, but when rumors started circulating about a Sasquatch, I started to see my experience in a different light."

"I can believe that."

"Thank you."

"What ever happened to Hiram?"

"He lived in that old shack until he passed away in his seventies. We became rather close. I wasn't afraid of him like some were. Maybe I should've been sometimes. We had a few close calls when he was in a bad way, but you know me."

Yes, Lindsay did know her.

"He and my father never spoke. I don't think I ever heard either man acknowledge that the other even existed. It all sounds very strange now, but I didn't realize that there was anything particularly unusual about the arrangement until I was in my teens. I can still remember the day I understood why he was out there. It's devastating when one comes to know that there are things that can happen to a person that the human heart is not equipped to bear."

Chapter Seven

In Which the Plot Becomes Thicker Than Figgy Pudding

By the time dinner was prepared and eaten and their guests were settled in for the night, Lindsay was ready to tip over with fatigue. She and Grace waited until Grandma was asleep and then tiptoed into the living room, where they hoped they wouldn't be overheard. The colored lights of the Christmas tree illuminated their faces with a cozy glow. Pale embers flickered in the fireplace. Both sisters were pajama clad. Grace climbed into an oversized chair and Lindsay wrapped herself in a fuzzy blanket on the couch, dumping a few of the pillows onto the floor.

Grace had been brought up to speed when it came to the Bigfoot hunters, as she had gotten to meet them at dinner that night. The men reported on all they had learned at the grocery store, which as it turned out was quite a lot. According to Mrs. Martel, half the village had spotted Bigfoot in fields, forests, and barns over the past eighty years. He had been suspected of pilfering chickens and swiping pails of milk. Grace was enthralled, practically begging to come along on their expedition the next day, and of course she was welcomed with open arms.

All that was left to discuss was Lindsay's meeting with Steve. She had tried not to think about it too much until now, which of course meant that she had been thinking of almost nothing else and didn't know where to begin.

"So he's asked you to take him back?" Grace asked.

"He wants to come around every now and then. I'm not completely sure what he's envisioning. I imagine he wants to help out with the inn and see if we can find our way back to each other."

Grace folded up her legs, cupped her chin in her hand, and looked thoughtful. "What did you say?"

"I said I'd think about it."

"Are you really considering this?"

"I think so. He claims he didn't try to start the barn on fire...that sounds crazy. Is this crazy?"

"I don't know. I mean, we were both afraid of him. We didn't know what he was up to. He didn't answer your calls for months...You know what? I'm sorry, but I do know. He left, completely out of the blue and without a trace. He cheated on you. He tried to burn down our barn. He was never nice to you. I can't think of any good reason to go along with a single one of his requests."

Wow. Maybe she should've anticipated that response, but for whatever reason Lindsay was dumbfounded. She didn't expect her sister to react to strongly. Grace was clearly upset; Grandma had been too. It seemed like they'd never liked Steve, but had held back for Lindsay's sake.

"I know all that," said Lindsay. "And before I saw him, I would've said there wasn't a chance I would even consider this. He was so downtrodden though, and he's still my husband. What if he was struggling with something that he's finally overcome, and I just shut him out?"

Grace got up and added another log to the fire, nestling it amongst the embers. It caught and flames licked its sides. Light and shadow danced across her face. "It sounds like you'll feel guilty if you don't do what he's asking."

Lindsay couldn't deny it. "I think I will."

"I can't imagine having to make this kind of decision, but you don't have anything to feel guilty about. Steve wouldn't be in this position if he hadn't burnt his bridges...pun intended. That was his choice. He wants you back, and he's upset he can't have you."

"I know I shouldn't feel responsible for him any more, but I do. It's not something I can turn off that easily. I haven't made up my mind either way. I'm thrown by how tempted I am to let him back in, though."

Lindsay had a sense of inevitability about it all that terrified her. Even as she spoke, she could sense that, whether it was tomorrow or next month or a year from now, she and Steve would slowly go back to the way they were, for good or for ill, ill being the most likely outcome.

"It's hard to let go of a person who's been such a big part of your life, but it's not going to get any easier, and I don't see him changing. Maybe I'm wrong. I didn't see him the other day, but my gut says it's time to let him go."

"Mine does too, but it's not that simple."

Grace looked like she was tempted to say more but shrugged her shoulders in resignation instead. There was nothing else she could say that Lindsay didn't already know.

"There's something else I wanted to talk to you about," said Grace, looking solemn. "I wasn't going to tell you tonight, but..."

"Oh. Ok." Lindsay waited.

"Betsy's pregnant."

Lindsay had been examining a hole in her fuzzy socks, but she stopped and looked up in shock. "What? How long have you known?"

"She told me last week. She just found out herself. It's George's."

"George's? Didn't he skip town?"

"He did. Betsy doesn't know why, but she thinks Chloe might."

"Because she's dating his twin brother."

"Right," said Grace. "And to answer your other question, no, George doesn't know. He hasn't been in touch with Betsy at all since he left. The whole thing is a mess."

"What will she do? George just disappeared on her."

"That's the problem. Betsy doesn't know where to turn," Grace said. "She's only told her sister, and I don't think Chloe's even told Arthur yet. What do you think?"

This was all too much. "I'm going to need more time to consider that one too. Is Betsy alright?"

"She seems alright. I think she'll be fine no matter what happens with George. Her family will be there for her, and all of us will too."

"But she's not sure about George's potential as a father."

"Not at all."

Between limping along with next to no information about the whereabouts of one's husband while trying to run a bed and breakfast and being pregnant with the child of a man who had fled town with the reputation of being a shady real estate developer at best and a thief at worst (if the rumors could be believed), there was very little substantial difference, and Lindsay had difficulty in deciding who had drawn the short straw, her or Betsy. Both of them, she supposed.

"I think we've both found ourselves in a bit of a conundrum," she said.

"Yes you have."

"Well, I'm not making any decisions about Steve for a while. He's going to have to get used to being the one who has to wait for me for a change."

"That's the spirit."

"Thanks, Grace. You can imagine what Grandma said about all this."

"Oh yes. And I have to admit, I probably agree with her."

Lindsay chuckled, but it emerged dry and sad. "The thing is, I agree with her too. As far as Betsy goes though, I think she should talk to Chloe. Even if Chloe knows something she can't share, she could steer Betsy one way or another."

"She's tried. Chloe won't say anything at all."

"Do you want me to try to talk to her?"

"Would you? I hate to ask, but Chloe will probably be more open with you. People tell you everything."

"Me? No they don't."

"Sure they do. Strangers are always coming up to you and telling you their life stories. People can sense your compassion. Some people, who shall remain nameless, may even take advantage of that quality."

Lindsay looked at her phone. It was late, and she suspected that her new guests would be early risers. She also had a text from earlier in the night that she hadn't noticed before. It was from Harvey.

Still on for cookies tomorrow?

Lindsay set her phone on the arm of the couch. Harvey was sure to be asleep by now. She'd reply in the morning. Should she go? Was she being selfish? If she was even considering letting Steve back in, she should probably start spending less time with Harvey. Nothing had happened between them; they'd been friends for years, but what if he was the one sending her gifts?

"What's up?" Grace asked.

"I got a text from Harvey asking me to come over tomorrow night to make sugar cookies with him and the kids. What do you think?"

"I think you should go. I'll keep things going around here. You've gotten to have all the fun with the Sasquatch men. It'll be my turn."

Lindsay's heart surprised her by racing as she asked, "Do you think Harvey's interested in me? I don't want to lead him on."

Her sister didn't hesitate. "Yes. Of course he is."

She hadn't expected such a definitive response. "Really?"

"I can't believe you're surprised by this. How many times did he stop by to check on us or drop something off last week? And the way you two steal glances at each other...I almost never hear you laugh anymore unless he's around."

"Doesn't that mean I should steer clear of him for a while, until I sort out my feelings about Steve?"

"I don't see why you should. You two are friends."

"But what if those gifts are coming from him?"

"I see what you mean, but like I said, you're not doing anything wrong. Harvey's a friend. You haven't led him on, and I know he's not the kind of person to see things that way either. If you're always just friends, I see that being okay with him."

Lindsay groaned. "I'm getting too old for this. Let's go to bed." She got up and blew out the cinnamon candle on the coffee table. She unplugged the tree. Wavy dots of candy colored light disappeared in the window, opening the way for the stars in the night sky to shine through. The moon was full. Its watery glow melted over the lawn, overspread with a silvery sheath of snow. A fox slipped out from beneath a spruce tree and slunk between the logs of the split rail fence.

Chapter Eight

In Which a Ghost of Christmas Past is Unearthed

The following morning, Lindsay texted Harvey as soon as she thought he would be awake.

Would love to come over tonight. What time?

She paused before hitting send. Hurting him was the last thing she wanted to do. On the other hand, if Grace was wrong and he only thought of her as a friend, there was no harm in spending time with him and his family. They were both on their own over the holidays and could use the companionship. Grace had been right about one thing for certain: they made each other laugh. They enjoyed each other's company. What could be wrong about that? She jabbed the little arrow next to her message. There. She had sent it.

He replied right away. *We'll start at 5:30. Call when you're on your way?*

Perfect, she replied. *See you then.*

She pulled a quiche out of the oven and set a bowl of fruit salad on the table. Grace shuffled downstairs and helped her get the drinks ready. Minutes later, the whole crew-Brian, Hook, and Moose-were huddled around the table, digging into their food and strategizing. They were seasoned professionals with their own jargon and multiple contingency plans.

"Did you see Grandma up there?" Lindsay asked Grace.

"No. I think she's still…"

Grandma Vivian glided down the stairs in her snow ghillie suit. She had always been a small woman, and had shrunk a bit with age. The suit looked appropriate for a three hundred pound man, and she was maybe one hundred pounds if she stuffed her pockets with rocks.

"What do you think?" she asked, twirling around as if she wore a stunning ball gown.

"I think you're prepared for this mission," Brian said approvingly. He wiped his mouth with a cloth napkin and stood up from his plate, which had been scraped clean twice. Moose and Hook did the same. "What do you think ladies?" Brian asked, addressing Lindsay and Grace. "You ready to suit up?"

"We were born ready," said Grace.

"That's what I like to hear. Let's go."

The men brought down five suits, slipping into theirs and handing two to their hostesses. It was sweltering inside the suit, but it was also fun to wear. Strips of wavering fabric fluttered with their every move.

Brian snapped to attention and faced them. "Alright, a few guidelines before we go out: One: no matter what happens, stick with us. Two: our methods are highly confidential. In other words, whatever you see out there stays out there. Three: do not harm the creature under any circumstances. We have a tranquilizer gun if need be. We've never had reason to use it, but it is there for our protection. Any questions?"

No one spoke up. They pulled on stocking hats that matched their suits and clumped out the door and down the stairs. Skirting past the barn, they followed each other in single file through the sleeping orchard.

In summer, the cherry trees' broad leaves blocked the view of the swampy forest in the distance, but now, in the midst of winter, the spindly branches did little to obscure their view. Chickadees chattered to each other, hopping from branch to branch. A few cherries, left behind and blackened by frost, clung to the branches; the birds picked them off and flitted away. The forest, however, was dense and quiet. Little pine trees sprouted up beneath towering oaks and maples.

Brian was in the lead and Lindsay brought up the rear of their company. When they had maneuvered their way through the orchard, they reached a wide open field and clustered closer together. Brian stopped and tilted his head towards the forest.

"What are we listening for?" asked Vivian.

"Shh," he said. "I'm listening for vocalizations

or tree whacking."

"Tree whacking? What's that?"

"Sasquatch communicate with each other by hitting tree trunks with their palms. It makes a distinctive hollow thwaping sound. When we get into the forest, I'll imitate the noise with a bat."

"Do you ever get a response?"

"We have. We can't be certain this close to civilization, because a car backfiring or a gunshot make similar sounds, but we've gotten responses in places that were miles and miles from anywhere."

They marched closer to the forest. The men examined the ground all the way there. Lindsay assumed they were looking for footprints. Hook and Moose had stayed completely silent all the way out. Lindsay and Grace followed their lead.

"How did you ever learn about all this?" asked Vivian. Lindsay had been wondering the same thing.

"My uncle was a cryptid hunter," said Brian. "He was all sorts of things, but that was one of them. He taught me everything I know. That was back in the day before the internet. These young guys have it easy. These days you can look up anything you want to know, but back in the day we had nothing but word of mouth to go by. It was a challenge to find other people who were doing the same work."

"So is that how you found Hook and Moose? Online?"

"Nope. We found each other in the woods not too far from here, in northern Minnesota. I was whacking a tree and imagine my surprise when I got a response right back. I was beside myself, and so were they. We had a good laugh when we realized that we were just a bunch of guys taking turns hitting trees with a bat."

"But your uncle got you into this rigmarole?" Vivian asked.

"He sure did. I grew up in eastern Oregon. My uncle, he was my mom's brother, was like a father to me. My mom didn't always like that." He chuckled and shook his head. "He wasn't exactly what one would call on the up and up, but we were like two peas in a pod from the start. He was a rascal that one, always up to trouble. We'd walk through the grocery store sneaking "free samples", and that was dinner. He'd take me to the zoo by hoisting me over the fence and following behind."

"Ha! Sounds like my kind of guy," said Grandma.

"He and a group of friends saw a Sasquatch in the mountains of Oregon," Brian continued. "He was with some guys who were believers before he was. They were out camping one evening, just sitting around the campfire, when someone started throwing rocks at them from a nearby hill. Not the kind of guys who were going to take that lying down, they marched right up that hill, expecting to see a group of rowdies. What they ran into instead was a full grown Sasquatch. He took to his heels when he spotted them, and my uncle freely admitted that he and his buddies did the same. He went back to that spot again and again over the years, but he never had another sighting."

"And he brought you along with him?" asked Grandma.

"He did. We were a team for a while, but then he got hurt doing a motorcycle stunt. After that he couldn't do the kinds of things he'd been able to do before. He got kinda restless, fell in with a bad crowd. He ended up in jail at the end of his life. Unfortunate, but that's the way it was."

They had reached the forest. The shack would've been difficult to find without her, but now that Lindsay was here, she could lead them right to it. There was a blackberry patch out that way that she visited every August. If it had been challenging for her to point out its exact location on the map, it would be easy to find it here on the ground. She knew every tree, hill, and swamp in these woods.

Brian paused and pulled a short bat out of his backpack. He hit an oak with it and a resonant thwack rang out. He did it again. Receiving no response, they carried on. Lindsay took the lead and everyone followed in line behind her. They didn't speak anymore, seeming to have made a nonverbal agreement that from this point on they would continue in silence.

Lindsay picked along extra slowly, peeking back at her grandma from time to time. She seemed to be keeping up. They clambered over patches of rocks and pushed past low hanging branches. Lindsay pulled her suit free from a raspberry bramble and continued on her way.

By the time they arrived at the old shack, Lindsay was hot and sweaty. She pointed to the well-hidden structure and the men nodded, scraping their way closer. A gaping entrance was accessible with the removal of some vines, and they picked their way inside.

"Should we follow them?" Grace asked. Grandma hung back.

"Why don't you stay here with Grandma," Lindsay said. "I'll follow them in to make sure they don't damage anything or get hurt." Would her insurance cover cryptid hunters in a dilapidated shack? She doubted it.

It was dark inside, but the going was easier here because the roof had kept out most of the snow. Brian shone his flashlight around the room. The dirt floor was littered with cracked nuts and tattered brown leaves. It was empty of any sign that this had once served as someone's home.

Lindsay stood in the corner, watching them. Suddenly, Hook got on all fours and called out, "Over here. I think there's a footprint."

The other two men hurried over for a closer look. "I think you're right," said Moose.

Hook backed up, and Brian scanned his flashlight across the ground. There was some kind of impression in the earth, but Lindsay wouldn't have been able to say if it was a footprint.

Brian stretched out a length of measuring tape and nodded. "Excellent find. I think I see a midtarsal break here."

Moose pulled out his camera, taking photos from every angle. "It's unmistakable. Look at the size of it. Must be the biggest one we've ever come across."

They stepped gingerly now, scouring the ground for more prints. Brian ran his hands over the wall. "I'm feeling for hair," he whispered to Lindsay. "We've found plenty of hair without the follicles attached, but unfortunately that doesn't contain any DNA."

Hook bagged up some soil samples and all three men went outside, leaving Lindsay alone. She was about to go when she felt something unyielding beneath her foot. She scraped at the ground in the corner, revealing the surface of something metal. Was she alone? Yes. No one was in the entrance.

She swept away more dirt and what appeared to be the lid of a box came into view. It was grooved, with rusty hinges on top. Lindsay took off her mittens to get a better grip. The soil wasn't entirely frozen inside the shed, and she was able to dig around the box enough to pry it free from the earth. Dirt caked beneath her fingernails. The tips of her fingers reddened with cold.

She turned over the object in her hand. It was an old ammunition box. She recognized it right away, having one just like it in her attic that belonged to her great-grandfather. After dusting off more dirt, some of the writing on the side was still legible: *24 Rounds Chargers. 40 MM Gun Shells.*

Lindsay filled in the hole as well as she could and smoothed its surface with the side of her hand. She stood, holding the case close to her body. The oversized ghillie suit folded over it, hiding it from sight. Lindsay went outside. Grandma shivered and Grace pointed in the direction from which they'd come. Lindsay approached Brian and whispered, "We're going to head out. I assume you can find your way back."

"Of course. Thank you for your help. This has been most interesting." He didn't take his eyes off the tree trunk he was scanning with his magnifying glass.

The three women made their way out of the forest, staying silent until they had reached the field.

"What an adventure," said Grandma. Her cheeks were pink and she beamed from ear to ear. "Nothing like some new blood in town to help you see familiar places in a whole new way. Now let's get home and eat; those three inhaled that quiche like it was made of air. I'd been counting on eating some."

They headed for the orchard through the snow, the stiff box remaining concealed beneath Lindsay's shaggy arm.

When they made it back to the farmhouse, Lindsay ran to her bedroom without removing her suit. She knelt on the floor, setting the box down in front of her. It wasn't locked, but the latches were rusted shut. She lifted it up, testing its weight. It was much heavier than the empty box in the attic. She tilted it to one side and something bumped against one wall with a dull thud, something that had likely been hidden by Hiram before he died. Would it be alright if she opened it? Hiram may have wanted it buried for a reason. Then again, maybe he had distant relatives who would want whatever was inside.

Lindsay brought it into the bathroom and brushed more dirt into the sink. Going back into her room, she opened her armoire. The letter from Steve was inside, propped against a safe that held her marriage license. She set the ammo box beside them both and pushed the door closed, another dilemma stashed away for the time being.

Chapter Nine

In Which it's Cold Outside, Baby

T hat evening, Lindsay found herself in Harvey's
kitchen, preparing to make sugar cookies
with him and his kids. Outside it was dark, the
air so cold it felt as if it could shatter. Inside, however,
canister lights spread a warm glow over the kitchen
island where Maddie and James sat at wooden stools.
Harvey fumbled in the cabinet for his biggest mixing bowls while Lindsay admired the early Christmas
card photos that had been squeezed in on the front of
the fridge.

The refrigerator door contained an impressive
collection of pictures, magnets, and artwork, the lat-
ter all different vintages and all created by Maddie
and James. There was a comic book cover featuring a
flying superhero in blue spandex that Lindsay didn't
recognize. It nearly obscured a photo of James, age 4
or 5, jumping off the couch with his baby blanket tied
like a cape around his neck. A self portrait of Maddie,

her body a square with stick arms and legs, was held up by a *Nick's Plumbing: We repair what your husband fixed* magnet.

Maddie hopped down and pulled her poppy patterned apron off a hook on the wall. She opened up a recipe box and thumbed through the cards inside until she found the one she was looking for.

"Some crazy tot took a bite out of this," she said, holding up a tattered floral recipe card.

Her brother James laughed. "Dude, that crazy tot was you."

"Um...no it wasn't."

"Who did it then?"

"Not me, that's for sure."

Harvey plucked it from her hand, lining it up with his mouth. "This seems like something I would've done, but the bite marks are a little too small."

"Maybe Lindsay did it," said Maddie.

Harvey held it up to Lindsay's face and she laughed. "Nah," he said. "Still too small. Must've been a mouse."

"I'm telling you..." said James.

His dad gave him a look, and James let it go with a shrug. Maddie had already moved on to creaming the butter and sugar anyway. She gripped the spoon with both hands and put her whole body into it.

"Can I crack the eggs, Dad?" she asked. James took over with the stirring while Maddie ran to the fridge to get the eggs. She expertly cracked two of them and set the runny shells on the table. "Do you want to crack one, Lindsay? You haven't gotten to help yet."

"Sure, I'd love to," she said. She cracked it on the side of the bowl and opened the shell with one hand, letting the gooey egg plop into the buttery mixture.

"Whoa. My mom could do that."

"I know she could," said Lindsay. She inspired me to learn how to do it. She always looked so stylish during the holiday bake-off, with her professional baking skills. She was my biggest competitor, you know."

"And she always won."

"You're right. She got first prize every year. She even made these sugar cookies once. Now I know her secret recipe."

Maddie gasped and put her hand over her mouth. "Don't tell anyone."

"I won't. I promise."

Gammy's Sugar Cookies was written across the top of the recipe card in a pretty hand. The little bite had removed some of the measurements, and Harvey wrote them in with a different colored ink. The card was splotched and wrinkled. It told the story of a happy family with a rambunctious toddler who had grown up to be a vibrant nine-year-old girl. Leah would've been so proud of her kids and how they'd grown. Lindsay couldn't believe she'd been gone for six years already.

Leah had been a forester, like Harvey. She

moved to town after they married, and she and Lindsay had become instant friends. Both women shared a love of baking and horses. They used to ride on the Ahnapee State Trail together, trotting through evergreen glades, farm fields, and prairies. Leah would point out all the native flowers when they popped up in the spring.

"Lindsay? Did you hear me?" Maddie asked.

"Oh. Sorry, what did you say?"

"Could you teach me to crack eggs like that?"

"Of course. Let's practice while the cookies bake."

Maddie nodded happily and poured the milk and vanilla with gusto. James jumped backwards to avoid being splashed, then went back to stirring.

"What are you making for the bake-off this year?" Harvey asked as he grabbed the flour from the pantry.

"I wasn't planning on doing it," said Lindsay. "I don't think I'll have time."

"What?" Maddie chimed in. "You *have* to do it. It won't be the same without you. Who will I cheer for?"

"She has a point," said Harvey, grinning. "You're going to let down your cheering section."

"And your eating section," Maddie added, scooping the flour into the bowl. She stopped. "I'm not sure how many cups I added."

"That was two," said James.

"Okay, three, four."

Harvey sat down at the table next to Lindsay.

"You're an incredible baker. It really wouldn't be the same without you. It's fun to watch you create those crazy elaborate desserts. You'll have some stiff competition this year, though. I hear Mrs. Martel is throwing her hat in the ring."

"Really? She's a legend among the Emma's Cafe Holiday Bake-Off contenders. Now I'm tempted to do it."

"It would be a pretty big deal-the current reigning champion versus the old time baking icon."

"Do it. Do it. Do it," Maddie chanted.

"Alright, if you all insist." Lindsay was touched. She hadn't been aware that she had such an ardent fan base.

"We do," said James. He adored Lindsay's cooking.

"I'm going to need to start thinking about what to make." Maybe there was a good reason that she had made that buche de Noel for Mrs. Johnston. It had turned out perfectly. If she decided on baking that for the competition, her practice was already complete.

The dough, having been mixed, was put in the fridge to cool for an hour. Maddie ran out of the room and came back with a pile of board games.

"Who wants to play?" she asked.

Harvey and Lindsay volunteered. James said he was going to head upstairs to work on a graphic novel that he'd been writing.

"It's so funny," he said. "You guys can read it when I'm finished."

Maddie chose one of the games and set it up while explaining the complicated rules. Lindsay tried to follow her instructions and hoped she could figure it out as they went along. Games had come a long way since the days of Clue and Monopoly.

Lindsay did catch on as they played. Maddie won. Harvey made a big show of being shocked that his brilliant strategy hadn't worked, but Lindsay suspected that he may have thrown the game at the end. They had time for one short card game before the dough was ready. Maddie turned on the back porch light before sitting down to play.

"It's snowing you guys," she said.

Sure enough, huge clumps of flakes drifted down from the night sky. From the looks of things, it had been going like that for a while.

"I didn't know it was supposed to snow, did you?" Lindsay asked Harvey.

"No. That's odd. Must be a little pop-up storm. It'll stop soon. I'll help you brush off your car before you leave."

They played their card game then called James to see if he wanted to help cut out the cookies. He did. Lindsay was impressed with their elaborate collection of cookie cutters. There were angels, Santas, elves, trees, bells, and even one shaped like Wisconsin.

"This one is my favorite," Maddie said, holding up a pudgy snowman.

"Maybe you'll be able to make a real snowman tomorrow," said Lindsay. "It's warm enough that the snow should be packy."

"Yes! I haven't made him this year. His name is always Snowman von Snowman."

"He sounds very noble."

"Yup. Big too. My dad has to lift the snowballs because they're *huge*. Do we have any carrots Dad?"

"We do, but I don't think we have any coal. Did you get any in your stocking from Saint Nick?"

"No. I'd never."

"I got some," said James, "but it was made of chocolate."

"Hmm...a warning," said Maddie. "Makes sense."

They slid the first batch of cookies into the warm oven. It didn't take long before they were ready to come out. They were a crisp golden brown and smelled heavenly. Maddie munched on one as they cut another sheet full.

"Let's practice the egg trick," she said.

"Alright." Lindsay took the eggs back out of the fridge and demonstrated the technique. Maddie tried to imitate her. She was cautious at first, and the egg didn't crack. The second time she made an attempt, she used plenty of pressure, so much so that the runny yolk ran down the sides of the bowl, leaving a gooey mess inside and out. Not to be deterred, Maddie kept trying until she had it down. She declared herself an expert after successfully cracking three eggs in a row into the bowl with one hand.

"As an added bonus, we can have scrambled eggs for breakfast before school tomorrow," said Harvey. He wiped down the bowl and covered it before setting it on a shelf in the fridge. "And speaking of school, it's getting late. I always forget how long it takes just to make the cookies. We'd better decorate them tomorrow night."

"Awww. But Lindsay won't be able to help then. Can you come back?"

"I'd love to, but I'll have to check with Grace. We have a group of Bigfoot hunters at the inn this week and they're quite a handful."

"No way," said James. "Are you serious?"

"I am. We even got to go out with them today." She told them all about the adventure.

"That's so cool. I wonder if they'll find anything. A kid at school said his dad said that his cousin saw one this fall when he was hunting."

"You never know what could be hiding in the woods," said Lindsay.

"On that note, you two run up and brush your teeth, and I'll be there in a minute to tuck you in." Harvey guided his kids towards the steps.

"You need to put three kisses under my pillow," Maddie reminded her dad. "You too, Lindsay." She ran upstairs.

"Do you want a hot chocolate before you go?" Harvey asked Lindsay.

"I'd love one."

Harvey took out a saucepan and started warming up milk on the stove while Lindsay carried bowls to the sink. They both sat down at the table. Harvey pulled off his sweater and rolled up the sleeves of his plaid shirt. He ran his hand through his wavy brown hair. It was getting long. Lindsay liked the look. It matched his stubbly beard and wind roughened skin.

"Maddie's been bouncing off the walls since she found out you were coming over tonight," he said.

"So have I. You guys are too funny. I just love it here."

He smiled at her and his smile was so open and unself-conscious that Lindsay couldn't help but smile back. He held her gaze; she didn't look away. The milk on the stove hissed and Harvey jumped up to take it off the burner. He stirred in the cocoa powder and sugar and poured it into two fat red mugs.

Maddie came back into the kitchen in her nightgown. A trace of toothpaste stuck to the corner of her mouth.

"Ready to be tucked in?" her dad asked.

"Almost. Can I have a glass of water with ice?"

Harvey filled up a glass at the sink and handed it to her. She wiped her mouth and said, "Will Lindsay read me a story?"

"I'd be happy to," she said, getting up from her chair. Maddie took her hand and led her upstairs into her bedroom. Harvey followed behind to check on James, who would already be in bed with a book.

"What story do you want?" Lindsay asked.

Maddie, who had already climbed into bed, leaned out and grabbed a thick pop-up book from the floor. It was *The Night Before Christmas*. Lindsay took it from her and opened it to the first page. It was incredibly detailed and elaborate. Sugar plums danced over the children's heads while their parents settled in for their warm winter's nap in a three dimensional bed. Their windows opened onto a snowy yard covered with new fallen snow.

When Lindsay got to the end, "And to all a good night," she closed the book and looked over at Maddie. She had fallen asleep, her dark blonde hair cascading over the pillow. Lindsay kissed her cheek and switched off the lamp next to her bed.

She tiptoed down the stairs and met Harvey back at the table. Their cocoa had gotten cold, and Harvey reheated their mugs in the microwave. Just as he was setting her drink back in front of her, Lindsay's phone rang.

It was Grace. "Hey, what's up?" Lindsay asked.

"You're not on your way back, are you?"

"Not yet. I'll be on my way soon though."

"Don't even think about it. Have you seen the roads?"

Lindsay hadn't. They hadn't looked outside since Maddie turned on the porch light over an hour ago. She flipped it on again. It was a total white-out. The friendly fluffy flakes were whipping in the wind and drifting against the sliding glass door.

"Wow. I had no idea," said Lindsay.

"Please don't try driving home. Everything's fine here. The guys go to bed early and Grandma's on a roll. She wouldn't let me into the kitchen before dinner tonight and you should've seen what she cooked up."

"Thanks for checking on me."

"No problem. It might be kind of nice, snowed in with Harvey..."

Lindsay stood up and walked away from the table. Could he hear her sister's side of the conversation?

"Thanks again," Lindsay said loudly. "I'll be in touch tomorrow."

"Sounds good. I just had the news on and they said it should be over by late morning, but school's cancelled already."

"I'll tell Maddie and James. Good night."

She came back to the table and told Harvey the news.

"Don't tell the kids tonight," he said. "James'll be too excited to sleep."

"I won't. I promise. I wouldn't want to rob him of that snowy morning feeling when your parents tell you that you can go back to bed."

"Bea and I never did stay in bed. We'd gulp down some cereal and run outside to play in the snow."

"That sounds just like Grace and me."

"Well, it looks like you're going to be staying overnight..."

"Looks like it..."

"It's like that song, *Baby it's Cold Outside.* I mean, sort of, you know." Harvey cleared his throat. "We have the guest room all set up for holiday visitors."

"Perfect. The guest room will be perfect." Lindsay gulped down her cocoa. "The kids seem ready for Christmas."

"Oh, they are. Maddie insists she's going to see Santa this year. Last year, she swore that he came into her room while she was still awake and put candy canes on her little tree, but she was too afraid to peek out from under her covers."

"I'm guessing she's developed a plan."

"She has, and it's an elaborate one. I'm not sure that she'll sleep at all Christmas Eve."

"Are they asking for anything special?"

"James wants a couple of new video games and some books. No surprise there. Maddie's been asking for a horse, but I'm not sure that we're ready yet."

"It's funny you should mention that, because Grace was just asking me why I didn't have horses anymore. I miss them, but they're a lot of work. They get into trouble if they're not being entertained."

"What about you?" he asked.

"I don't absolutely have to be entertained, but it helps."

He laughed. "I hope I'm doing a decent job of entertaining you then. I wouldn't want you getting into trouble."

"You're doing a great job," she said.

"But really, is there anything you're hoping for?"

Lindsay thought about it. No one had asked her that question this year. Come to think of it, no one had asked her that question for as long as she could remember. Steve usually got her something practical, like a vacuum cleaner or a toaster. It made sense; their appliances wore out quickly, but it was nice to be asked. She wished she had an inspired answer.

"I'm not really sure." Should she mention the gifts from her secret admirer? No. If they were from him, he might be embarrassed. If they weren't, it would be awkward that she brought it up. "I drink a lot of tea. There's this banana chocolate kind that I love. I guess that's pretty simple, but it's my favorite thing."

"Simple is the best," he said.

"What about you? Is there anything you want for Christmas?"

"There is…" He smiled at her again and, once again, she couldn't help but smile back.

Finally, she asked, "What is it?"

"That's between me and St. Nick. If I tell you, I might not get it."

"I thought that only applied to birthday wishes."

"Hmm…I don't think so. I'm pretty sure it applies to Christmas ones too."

"Does that mean I won't get my wish?"

"No. I'm certain you will," he reassured her.

"Okay. Fair enough."

"I can tell you one of my minor wishes, though."

"Why, thank you." She laughed as he worked to look comically serious.

"I'm hoping for banana chocolate tea so I can tempt you to come over more often."

"Really?"

"Well, yes, that would be a good start, but I'd also like some warmer mittens. People keep giving me gloves, because I work outside, which makes sense, but my hands are always freezing. Some magical warm mittens would be just the thing."

"Santa has his work cut out for him over here. I hope you get what you're wishing for," she said.

"Thanks," he said. "Me too."

Chapter Ten

In Which Snow is Glistening in the Lane

Lindsay had forgotten to close the blinds the night before, and although the storm had weakened considerably, snow continued to fall outside her bedroom window. She stretched and got out of bed, pushing aside the lace curtains that helped filter out some of the early morning sunlight. Judging from the pile on the picnic table, a foot and a half or more of snow had been dropped on their little village, with drifts like frozen waves that overspread the icy fields.

She couldn't wait to hear the kids' reaction to their unexpected snow day. Maybe they could frost their sugar cookies before they headed outside to play. Pulling on her jeans, Lindsay nudged open the door and listened. It didn't sound like anyone else was awake yet. She tiptoed down the hallway and opened the bathroom door, slipping inside and closing it behind her.

She turned around to behold Harvey, stepping out of a steamy shower and ruffling his hair dry with a towel. She gasped and he looked up, startled. He tossed the towel around his waist. Lindsay covered her face and backed into the door then peeked between her fingers to talk to him.

"I'm so sorry. I didn't know you were in here." She backed up, reaching for the doorknob, when a knock came from the hallway.

"Lindsay? Is that you?" It was Maddie.

Lindsay lowered her hands and turned back to Harvey with wide eyes. "Yes. It's me," she called. "I had to stay overnight in the guest room because of the big snowstorm."

"Were you yelling in there?"

"I was, yes. I saw….a mouse. I saw a mouse but it ran away. Everything's alright."

"It's probably the one that bit the cookie card."

"Could be."

Harvey shoulders shook in silent laughter. Lindsay wanted to join him but was so mortified that she couldn't bring herself to do it. She tried to look at anything but the dripping towel-clad man in front of her, but the room was tiny, even by old farmhouse standards. The towel wasn't all that big either.

Lindsay stepped closer to him, still averting her eyes, and whispered, "What should we do?"

"Tell her you were just about to get in the shower, and you'll meet her downstairs."

Why hadn't she thought of that? She was flustered, that's why. Harvey didn't seem flustered at all, just a little chilly. He hugged his arms and rubbed them, but the towel slipped; he grabbed it before it could fall to the floor.

"I'm going to take a shower, but I'll be down right after that," said Lindsay.

"Okay," Maddie yelled. She ran down the steps, likely headed for the kitchen and her expertly cracked eggs.

Lindsay turned around, peering out into the hallway. The coast was clear. She whispered, "Sorry," one last time and sneaked out of the bathroom.

When Lindsay reached the kitchen, she found Maddie, pulling the bowl of eggs out of the fridge. The frying pan was on the stove, a block of cheese on the table.

"I thought you were taking a shower," said Maddie.

"I was going to, but I changed my mind. Hey, it's a snow day. You don't have to go to school."

Maddie's jaw dropped. She did a little dance around the kitchen. "I'm going to tell James," she said, boogying over to the stairs.

"Let him sleep. We'll get breakfast ready and surprise him."

Maddie stopped in her tracks and turned around. She pulled out a whisk and whipped the eggs. Lindsay found the cheese grater and got to work on shredding the sharp cheddar. By the time the guys came downstairs, the table was set with four plates full of bacon, scrambled eggs, toast, and cantaloupe.

"Now this is a breakfast fit for a snow day," said

Harvey. He acted as though nothing out of the ordinary had happened, and Lindsay followed his lead.

James agreed. His wrists stuck out beyond the sleeves of his striped pajamas, and his stylish haircut was rumpled and pushed over to one side, making him look more like a little boy than a young man.

"Can we frost our cookies after breakfast?" Maddie asked.

"Of course. This snowstorm couldn't have been timed any better if we'd planned it." Harvey smiled and took a bite of his eggs. Lindsay silently agreed with him.

"Is Lindsay going to stay?"

"You'll have to ask her," he said, "but I think she might have to. The snowplow hasn't come through yet."

"Of course I'll stay," said Lindsay, "at least as long as we're snowed in. I want to meet Snowman von Snowman."

"Awesome," said Maddie.

After they'd finished breakfast, Lindsay brought out the cookies. Harvey whipped up some vanilla frosting, James grabbed the sprinkles, and they got to work. James decorated slowly and deliberately, using a toothpick to dot sprinkles onto the frosting. His snowmen wore striped scarves. Holly berries and leaves adorned bells and wreaths. Maddie took the opposite approach, glopping on the frosting with reckless abandon and then shaking sprinkles over the cookie, her plate, and the table.

By the time they had decorated all of the

cookies, it was late morning. The snow had nearly stopped, but the plow still hadn't come through. Lindsay's phone rang from inside her purse by the back door. She moved to grab it, then took a look at her sticky hands and ran to the sink to rinse them off. By the time she reached her phone, it had stopped ringing.

It was Grace, and it looked like she'd missed an earlier call from her as well. She listened to her messages.

Lindsay? I'm in the garage trying to start the snow blower. It's not working. Is there a trick to it or something? The guys want to leave, but they're stuck. Call me back.

Still out here. If you get this, call me right away. Brian's chomping at the bit. They're going to start trying to shovel themselves out. Also, Grandma's driving me mad. I don't think I can hold her off from trying to shovel with them. Help!

How could Lindsay explain how to start the snow blower? It was fifty years old and, yes, there were several tricks to getting it to start. Even with the tricks, it only started half the time. Why hadn't she thought to get a new one before a big storm hit?

She called Grace back. "Hey. Did you figure it out?"

"Not even close. Where did you get this thing?"

"Rummage sale. I know; it's ancient. It's going to be impossible for me to explain how to start it without having it in front of me, and even then I can't guarantee that it'll work. I haven't used it since last

March."

"You seriously need a new one."

"Yes. Thank you."

"Don't get snippy with me. You're not the one stuck in the house with Grandma and three antsy lodgers."

"Sorry. I'm just frustrated with myself." Lindsay went into the living room and looked outside. She could see Bea's family farm across the road. The county highway hadn't been plowed yet. "I'm still stuck here."

"What should I do?"

"I'm not sure. Don't let Grandma shovel. I'll call you back in a minute." She hung up and went back into the kitchen where Harvey was wiping up sprinkles. The kids had run off to get ready to go outside.

"Hey. Is Grace alright?" he asked.

"She can't get the snow blower to run, and our guests want to start their morning adventure."

"I can run over with my truck. I just put the plow on it."

"That's so nice of you, but the road's not clear yet."

"Okay. Well, let her know that whenever it is, I'll run over. Would you mind staying here with the kids? They're alright on their own, but I think they'd like it if you'd get out there with them."

"I wouldn't have it any other way," said Lindsay. "And thank you for helping again. I feel like I've been monopolizing your time."

"Not at all. I want to help, really. I've seen your

snow blower, though. You should get a new one."

"So I've heard," Lindsay chuckled. "I'll get right on that." How much did a new snow blower cost? She had no idea. She should've been looking for them over the summer, instead of being one of the masses who was going to try to get one after the first big snow. She'd be lucky to find one at all at this point, and no one was going to be offering them at a bargain.

"As long as we're stranded, we might as well make the most of it," said Harvey. "I'm guessing you don't have snow gear?"

"I do, actually. Or, I have boots in my car anyway."

"Let me grab them for you," he said. "That way you won't have to wade out there in your shoes."

"Hey Harvey, sorry about…well, you know." Lindsay was sure her face was turning redder than Rudolph's nose.

"Don't think twice about it. I'm the one who should've locked the door."

He stepped outside, trudged his way to the car, and grabbed her boots from the back seat. The snow was piled up so high that her door just barely cleared it.

In the meantime, Lindsay called Grace to let her know that Harvey would get there as soon as he could.

"Tell him thank you from me. He's literally saving a life here, either mine or Grandma's. I practically had to wrestle her to keep her from going out there this morning."

"I'll tell him," said Lindsay. "It shouldn't be long."

When he got inside, Harvey offered Lindsay a pair of oversized snow pants. She pulled them on just as the kids ran into the kitchen. All of them geared up and raced outside. James was determined to make the biggest snowball ever for the base of their snowman. He rolled the ball until he couldn't push it any longer. As predicted, the snowman's middle was so big that Harvey had to lift it, with Lindsay's help. He heaved it as high as he could but had to roll it to its final perch atop the massive base. The head was much easier to make and lift.

When they were finished, the snowman and Harvey were about the same height. Maddie ran inside to get a carrot for the nose and a scarf to wrap around his neck. James found two long sticks and stuck them into the middle ball for arms. Because no one had earned real coal that year, Maddie grabbed some rocks near the foundation of the house and used them to fashion eyes, a mouth, and buttons.

"I'm going to have to be bad next year so we can get our hands on some real coal," she said. Maddie looked off into the distance with a grin on her face that said that she was rather looking forward to seeing what kind of mischief she was capable of.

"I don't know if that's necessary," said Harvey. "We could just ask Santa for some. I'm sure he has extra."

Maddie shrugged, leaving Lindsay with the feeling that she preferred going the naughty route.

Just as they had finished their snowman, the plow roared by, leaving a trail of rock salt behind it.

"I'm going to rescue Grace," said Harvey. "You kids be good for Lindsay, alright?" Maddie grinned wickedly. "You don't need to start earning coal quite yet, Maddie," he added.

"Fine," she said, but her grin snapped back into place the second her dad's back was turned.

"Thank you," said Lindsay. "I'm so grateful, and I know Grace will be too."

"Anything I can do to help is great by me," he said, and left to save the day.

"What do you want to do next?" Lindsay asked the kids.

"Let's build a fort," James suggested.

"Yes! Let's make two forts and have a snowball fight," his sister said.

They set to work, James creating a fort on his own while Lindsay and Maddie crafted one nearby. Both kids were impressed with their guest's fort building skills.

"Grace and I built forts out in the orchard all the time when we were little. She's the real expert. We'll have to get her out here some time so she can show you her techniques."

Maddie loved that idea. She rolled snowballs all over the yard, and Lindsay carried them to be added to their fort. They hadn't been working long when Harvey returned.

"That was quick," said Lindsay. "How's everything looking over there?"

"It was actually already done by the time I got there. Grace had tried calling you back, but I told her you were outside."

"Who had done it?"

"Dave Anselme."

"Officer Anselme? Really?"

"I know. Grace looked really pleased. She said he had just happened to be passing by in his truck."

"Hmm...that's interesting. We don't get much traffic out that way."

"I thought the same thing."

"Sorry you drove all the way out there for nothing, though."

"It was no big deal. Grace said to tell you that everything's spiraling out of control, but you should stay here for lunch."

"Is that what she really said?"

"No. She said everything's fine. The guys had already left by the time I got there. She really did say you should stay though. Apparently our helpful officer is sticking around for lunch at your house, and your grandma took off with the hunters."

"I see. Well, this is all making a lot of sense now. I'd be happy to stay for lunch, if you'll have me."

"Yes! You have to stay," said Maddie. "Grilled cheese for everyone!" She spun around and flopped back into the snow, flailing her arms to make a wild snow angel. James lobbed a snowball at them from behind his impenetrable fortress and Lindsay's second snowball fight of the season was on.

Chapter Eleven

In Which Lindsay Receives Tidings of Great Joy

L indsay got home just in time to pass Dave Anselme on his way home from having lunch with her sister. His dark reflective glasses usually made him look stern and serious, but he had been singing as he made his way down the road.

Lindsay found Grace in the living room, playing with a tiger striped kitten. The kitten tugged on the tree skirt with all its might then spun in a circle and pounced. Grace wiggled one of the lower branches, jiggling the ornaments, and the kitten tried to stand on its hind legs to swat a dangling ball. It tipped over backwards and wriggled around to try again.

"Where did this guy come from?" Lindsay asked.

Grace looked up. "Oh. You're back. You're not going to believe it. She's your latest present." The kitten had gone back to tugging on the tree skirt and Grace picked her up and snuggled her in her lap.

"Are you serious?"

"Absolutely. There was a kitten, food, dishes, a litter box, toys, everything."

Lindsay was taken aback. This was a bit much. She wasn't sure if this was quite what she needed right now. She watched the little scamp leap out of Grace's lap and go after the tree skirt for a third time. Both sisters laughed. Grace stood and handed her a note.

Delight and joy to my very favorite person at Christmastime. Love, Your secret admirer

Lindsay leaned down to ruffle the tiny animal's fuzzy fur. "When did she show up? Haven't you been snowed in?"

"I found her right after Harvey left. She had a tag on her neck that said her name was Joy, but I had to take it off because she kept tying herself in knots trying to get to it. I hope you don't mind that I read your note. It looks like your secret admirer has struck again."

"If she showed up right after he left, it's probably Harvey, right? But how would he have hidden away a kitten? I was with him all morning."

"I'm not sure. It's a Christmas mystery."

"Should I ask him about it?"

Grace considered. "I probably wouldn't yet, in case it isn't him."

"You're right. I just can't imagine who else it could be though. Did you see anyone else this morning? Other than your handsome officer, I mean."

"I didn't, and I've been meaning to talk to you about that."

"About Dave?"

"Yeah. We've been seeing each other for a while."

"I kind of guessed that."

"Did you know before, or did you just guess now?"

"I had no idea until this morning. It wasn't exactly difficult to put the pieces together. How long is a while though?"

"Just a month or two. I was going to tell you, but..."

Grace trailed off and Lindsay knew what she wasn't saying. Grace didn't want her sister to feel like the only one not paired up over the holidays. It was a thoughtful gesture, but she wished she didn't appear as fragile and distraught as she felt. She was used to being the one looking out for Grace, not the other way around.

"I'm really happy for you," said Lindsay. "He seems like a great guy."

"Thanks." Grace looked relieved. "He is. He just asked me to the New Year's party. He said he felt a little odd asking, given that we're hosting it, but he wanted to be my date. I said yes, of course."

"That's so sweet." Lindsay really was happy for her sister. When Grace had moved back home, Lindsay worried that there wouldn't be anything for her here, that she might come to regret it. Grace had been making the most of her return from the start though, reconnecting with her old friend Betsy, getting out to parks and festivals, and now finding a new boyfriend.

Maybe she'd be sticking around longer than either of them had initially planned.

"So, it looks like we have a kitten now," said Grace. Joy sprinted out of the room and could be heard sliding across the kitchen floor. Lindsay left and came back with the squirming bundle in her arms. She was adorable and soft, and possibly exactly what a historic bed and breakfast and its weary innkeeper needed.

The two sisters spent the rest of the afternoon acquainting Joy with her new home while trying to make dinner. It was a bit of a balancing act, and they took turns making sure the kitten didn't get into too much mischief.

Somehow, everything came together by the time darkness fell and Moose, Hook, and Brian returned. Grandma wasn't with them. "She met up with some friends while we were out doing interviews and headed to Emma's Café for dinner. Said to tell you she'd be back tonight," Brian informed them.

The men flopped down into the kitchen chairs. They were quiet while they ate, but stayed at the table afterwards and swapped stories about their day. It sounded as if they had split up for a while, in order to gather more stories from around town. They had several leads that they planned on following up on for the rest of the week.

Grace and Lindsay pretended not to be listening, but it took them an extra long time to clean up in the kitchen and prepare dessert that evening. It seemed that many other old-timers, people around

Grandma's age, had seen something out in the woods as children as well. Lots of them volunteered to let the hunters set up cameras and scour their part of the countryside for evidence.

"I'll tell ya," said Moose, "I've never felt closer than we are right now."

Hook agreed. "These people here, they're the genuine article. If we don't find definitive proof somewhere around here, I'm hanging up my hat for good and slinking back to Idaho."

"Ha!" Moose slapped his leg. "I'll believe that when I see it. But hey, Brian might even earn his name. You still holding out for Squatch, Brian?"

"Sure am."

Grace couldn't resist chiming in. "I wanted to ask. How did you two get your names? Moose? Hook?"

Hook scowled. "What do you mean, how'd we get them? Those are our names."

"I mean…oh, I'm sorry. They're great names. I didn't mean…"

He chortled at her horrified expression. "My name's not really Captain Hook, although I gotta say, Moose would be a pretty great name. They're our mountain man names. Got 'em when we were living rough in the mountains of Idaho."

"Tell 'em how you got yours," Moose said to Hook.

"Gladly, if they wanna hear it."

They did, Grace emphatically so.

"Alright, here goes: I was out fly fishing in a stream one day, all by my lonesome, and I hooked myself straight through the forearm." Hook pulled up the sleeve of his thick thermal shirt, pushed aside a thicket of dark arm hair, and revealed a smooth white scar on the top of his lower arm. "Had a bottle of Captain Morgan by my side, so I took a swig, splashed it on the hook, and yanked that sucker all the way through. It hurt like the blazes at first, but then I felt better and went on fishing.

"I acted so relaxed about it, that no one believed me when I went back to camp that night, not even with that nasty hole in my arm. So the next day, I went back out there with a posse of fellas and showed them what happened, and darned if I didn't go ahead and hook myself a second time. Them guys were no help at all. They were rollin' around on the ground laughin' like it was the funniest thing they ever saw. Well, I did it again. I poured that rum down my gullet and doused that hook and pulled it through. After that, everyone believed me of course, and I wisened up enough to decline any further offers to reenact my unfortunate accident."

Moose and Brian guffawed as if it was the first time they'd heard that story in their lives

"Didn't it get infected?" Grace asked. The nurse in her must've been horrified.

"Nope. Never did. I've kept a bottle of the Captain in my truck forever after, just in case. I swear by the stuff."

"You never landed yourself again, though. You should see him fish now," Moose said. "He practically tosses the line in and winces as he does it." He pantomimed a weak throw and laughed until he cried. Hook gave him a gentle whack over the head and laughed along.

"Hey, you would too, if you'd been in my predicament even once. Why don't you tell them how you got your name, then?"

Moose scoffed. "I faced down a lot more than a teeny hook."

"Go ahead."

"Gladly. I was living in the mountains, same as Hook here. I had an old pickup that I parked outside my abode. One morning I woke up, and a big ol' moose was standing there with one foot propped up on the hood, denting it. Well, I never saw a moose act like that before. I walked right up to it and told it to scoot. Informed it that that was my truck he was using as a step stool. It put its foot down, real gentleman-like, which I thought was fairly neighborly, so I went inside to get my camera.

"When I came back out and tried to get a picture, the moose developed an objection to my presence. He chased me, both our legs flailing, right back into the cabin. I pulled out my shotgun and waited in case he got the idea to come busting inside. When I looked out the window, he was walking in circles, shaking his head and bumping into trees. It was real strange, but I've seen sick animals before. I hated to do it…I had to shoot him, can't stand to see a beautiful animal suffering like that. I kept his antlers and got the name, too."

"It seems like there's a lesson here," said Grace

"Like you're taking something difficult that happened to you and turning it around so it becomes a positive part of..."

"Nah," said Hook, fiddling with the beads woven into his beard. "It's just funny. Brian here's had his fair share of numbskull moves too, but he's holding out to find a Bigfoot so he can earn the name Squatch. It's what he wants to be remembered for."

"Nothing wrong with that," said Brian. "My uncle never did have his proof." He gave the other two a pointed look, daring them to laugh. "I want people to know that he was searching for something real, even if he seemed like a rascal to most of them."

The mood had turned somber, but just then Joy raced by with a jingle ball stuck to her paw. She shook it until it flew under the table. The kitten scooted between the men's feet in hot pursuit.

"Whoa there," said Brian. "Where'd this little critter come from?"

"We don't know," said Lindsay. "Someone's been leaving me gifts on the back porch. Joy's the latest."

Brian reached under the table and picked the kitten up, cradling her in his arms. She swatted at his beard as he jostled her tummy. "Joy. I like that. Good mountain cat name."

"You think so?"

"Yep. If there's anything I know well, it's how to read animals, and you've got yourself a good one here. People can sometimes be a little trickier, but I don't think I'd be remiss to suggest that you're a good one as well. You two will get along just fine."

Later that night, so late that it nearly qualified as early the next morning, Lindsay lie in bed, unable to sleep. She rolled over and flipped on her lamp. Tossing off her quilt, she swung her legs out of bed and winced as her feet hit the cold wood floor. She stepped gingerly across the room until she reached the worn hand-tied rug before her armoire. It had been staring at her from across the room as she tried to fall asleep, and Lindsay was sure that the only way she could get it to leave her alone was to open it up and face the phantoms that lurked inside.

She pulled open the doors with a snap and they squeaked towards her. Beneath folded sweaters and scarves sat the ammo box and mementos of her married life. A shiny silver frame contrasted sharply with the dull rusty metal box. She picked up the frame and considered the couple in the photo. It was her and Steve, but so much had changed, inside and out, that she hardly recognized them. Steve was clean shaven, his face rounder and softer. Lindsay's curly chestnut hair was so long that the weight of it made it look almost straight.

They were on their honeymoon in Montana, standing on the side of a mountain pass. A distant lake with a pine filled island at its center blurred in the background. Lindsay recalled the moment before they took the photo. Steve was setting up his tripod. He had wanted to go to Hawaii, but Lindsay wasn't open to flying anywhere. It was late August, and snow had already begun to fall in the mountains of western

Montana. Neither of them had brought proper gear for the weather, and Lindsay shivered, anxious to hop back into the warm car. Right before the photo had been taken, Steve had said, "How do you like your fabulous honeymoon now?"

To anyone else, Steve and Lindsay would appear to be a young couple in love, but Lindsay could see the hurt and surprise in her eyes as she put on her smile for the camera.

She had said something to Steve about his comment afterwards, and how it made her feel. He insisted that he hadn't meant anything by it, that she was being overly sensitive. Even now, she questioned herself. Had he been joking? Was she too sensitive? Perhaps that was what had driven him away. The things he had done, leaving without a trace, turning to someone else, were wrong, but perhaps she had a bigger role in the demise of their marriage than she'd been willing to acknowledge. Steve often informed her, in the years to follow, that she had misunderstood him, that she was imagining things, making life difficult for both of them.

Shaking her head, Lindsay set the photo back on the shelf and lifted the weighty ammo box. When she tilted it this time the clang of something metal on metal broke the silence of the little room. She tried the latches again, but they wouldn't budge. She hadn't really expected them to. Shoving the box back into the armoire, Lindsay clicked the doors shut and hopped into bed, snapping off the lamp and pulling the quilt up to her neck. Her muddled thoughts kept her from sleep, and when she woke the next morning, she felt that her mind had never stopped working, that she had never really slept at all.

Chapter Twelve

In Which a Skating Party Takes a Frightful Turn

The next three days flew by in a whir of cleaning, cooking, and kitten wrangling. There were no big surprises, but that was only because Lindsay had come to expect the unexpected around here, what with Grandma haring to and fro, the lodgers tromping in with tall tales at all hours, and presents showing up daily on her back doorstep. So far, she'd received bath salts, a candle, and-this was interesting-a massive pouch of her favorite banana chocolate tea.

Now Lindsay was waiting for her sister to get back from work so she could meet her friends at the pond behind Wes's cabin for some ice skating. She picked up a musty washcloth and carried it into the basement to be tossed in with the rest of the towels.

Grace called from upstairs. "I'm home!"

Lindsay started the washing machine spinning

and met her in the kitchen. "Hey, how was work?"

Grace pulled off her coat and draped it over the back of a chair. She plopped into one seat and put her feet up on another. "It was really busy. The flu's starting to go around."

Lindsay brought her a mug of peppermint tea. Grace sipped it and closed her eyes. Suddenly remembering her sister's plans, her eyes popped open as she said, "You should go, everybody else is probably there already. How are you on skates? I don't think I've gone since we were kids."

"Same here. I picked up a pair a couple of years ago. They fit, so that's a start, right? Chloe's really good. She said she'd teach me a few moves."

Grace laughed. "I would love to see that." She grabbed a book that she'd hidden in the corner of the kitchen counter, behind a Santa cookie jar, and cracked it open. She dangled the bookmark at her side and Joy raced across the kitchen, pouncing at and expertly grabbing its golden tassel.

"Whoa. I didn't expect that kind of athleticism." Grace chased after the kitten to retrieve her bookmark. When she had gotten it back, disentangling the kitten's claws, she asked, "Did you ever get a chance to talk to Chloe about Betsy?"

Lindsay had completely forgotten. "I haven't. I'm so sorry," she said, pulling on her hat. "I know it's really important, but I've had a lot on my mind." That was an understatement. She still didn't know what to do about Steve, and had slept fitfully every night that week. She hadn't heard from him at all since his visit, which she took as a sign that he was respecting her need for space at least.

Grace nodded as if she understood. "Do you think you'll be able to talk to her today? Betsy's been asking."

"I'll try. Arthur will be there, so I'm not sure if it's the best time, but I promise I'll do my best."

"Thanks. I know it's not really our place, yours or mine, but Betsy's so in the dark about why George left."

"I understand. I'll ask her about it soon, but I'm not going to press if she doesn't want to talk."

"No. I wouldn't want you to. I just figured anything to give Betsy more clarity would be worth a shot."

Lindsay picked up her skates by the laces and made her way to her car. It hadn't snowed since the big storm. The driveway was clear for the time being. Lindsay had sought out a snow blower close to home, but everyone was sold out of the ones that she could afford. Perhaps she could get someone to look at the one she had. She gave it a glance. It was heavy, cumbersome, and cobbled together, but it was hers. She'd have to find a way to make the most of it until she could come up with something more reliable.

She drove past Arthur's farm and turned into the driveway that led to Wes's log cabin in the woods. In addition to the Door County Bookmobile, which Wes drove as the village librarian, Chloe's truck was parked in front of the garage. Merry voices floated over the cabin roof, and Lindsay followed them to the frozen pond where Wes, Bea, Chloe, and Arthur were skating. Chloe seemed to already have her teaching work cut out for her. Arthur tripped and wobbled as he made his way across the ice. He clutched Chloe's arm, nearly taking her down in the process.

Bea and Wes, however, looked like they had been born with skates on their feet. Actually, that wasn't too far from the truth. They'd been coming to the pond to skate since they were kids. Bea's farm was no more than a half mile down the road, and she and Wes had been inseparable until he moved away over a decade ago. Now that he was back, they'd picked up right where they left off. They glided beneath the bridge that spanned the pond, holding hands and laughing.

Oh well, at least Lindsay wasn't the only one who needed a good tutorial. She walked through the snow and sat down on the edge of the pond just as Bea glided up to her.

"I'm so happy you could make it," said Bea.

"Thanks. It looks like fun." Lindsay popped off her boots and wriggled her feet into her skates before lacing them up tight.

"I'll help you up," Bea offered, taking her hand.

Lindsay stood. The ice was smooth and so clear that she wouldn't have been surprised to see the wavering forms of fish and undulating seaweed down below. Once she started taking tentative steps, she found that she could glide a bit by shifting her weight from one foot to the other. She slowly made her way around the pond, brushing past the cedars that lined its shore. They blocked the wind that had whistled and buffeted the windows of her car on the drive over.

"Hey, you're pretty good," said Chloe, skating up next to her. "You claimed you didn't know how to skate."

"I don't," said Lindsay. "I'm just figuring it out as I go."

"Well, you look great from here. Keep up the good work."

"It looks like Arthur's new to skating too."

"He is, but he's been a great sport about it." Arthur was taking a break, having pulled off his skates. He was lounging in one of the chairs on the back porch and enjoying a steaming mug of hot chocolate.

Lindsay felt awkward asking about Betsy, but this was her chance, and she'd promised Grace she'd seize the moment if an opportunity presented itself. "Can I ask you about something?"

"Shoot." Chloe skated backwards in front of her.

"It's about Betsy."

"Oh." Chloe flipped around and slowed down so they were side by side. They travelled to the far end of the pond, away from everyone else, and stopped. "Do you know what I think you know?"

"Yes, I mean, I think so. Is Betsy really pregnant?" Lindsay whispered.

"She is." Chloe shot a glance around the pond. No one was within earshot.

"Obviously you don't owe me any information, but do you know something that might help her decide what to do?"

"I do, and I've been really conflicted, because it's not my place to share anything I know about George. What I do know, however, makes it pretty important that she doesn't think of him as someone to rely upon. I don't think a future with him, if that's even an option, would be a happy one."

"Have you told her that?"

"In so many words. She has to know that I wouldn't steer her wrong, but I'm sure there's a part of her that wants to believe that he's better than his press."

Lindsay understood that only too well. "Do you want to know what I think?"

"I do. I'll take all the advice I can get."

"I think Betsy should tell Sarah. Sarah's a realist. Even though George is her son, she'll help Betsy make a clear-eyed decision about when to tell him and how to involve him in her life. Sarah's already like a mother to all of us in the society; now she'll really be a grandma to Betsy's baby."

"I'm with you, and I think Betsy knows that would be for the best too, it's just taking her a while to work up the courage to do it...Oh my gosh. Look. I think Wes is about to propose."

Wes had stopped skating beside Bea and was kneeling down on the ice behind her. Bea hadn't noticed yet. He tied his laces and stood, hurrying to catch up with her. Lindsay and Chloe laughed.

"False alarm," said Lindsay.

The other two skaters reached them in no time.

"Let me in on the joke," said Bea.

"You had to be there," said Chloe.

"Want to come inside and warm up?" Wes asked.

Lindsay's ankles were tired and the tips of her toes ached with cold. She envisioned toasting her feet by the woodstove and sipping cocoa topped with mini marshmallows in Wes's cozy cabin. It was a no-brainer.

"I'm ready. How about you?" she asked Chloe.

"Me too. I think I speak for Arthur as well when I say that he's had enough." She waved to him and he waved back from his perch on the back porch. "Let's do this again soon though."

They all agreed and crossed the pond, gliding across its smooth surface. Lindsay was getting pretty good at this. Maybe she'd ask Chloe to teach her to skate backwards next time. She sped up, gliding forwards with ease.

She hit a bump and started to pitch forwards. Leaning backwards to counter her momentum, she wheeled her arms but it wasn't enough; she was going to fall with a smack onto the ice. She reached her arms behind her, trying to protect her butt and tailbone from a painful jolt. The shock assaulted her wrist instead, and she screamed in pain. Searing agony ripped up her arm. Gripping her throbbing wrist, she closed her eyes. The pain in her butt and hip where she had hit the ice faded into the background. She didn't move a muscle, shrinking into herself.

"Are you okay?" she could hear someone asking. She couldn't speak. She felt like she might be sick.

"I think I broke my wrist," she squeaked out from between clenched teeth.

"Do you think you can stand? If we can get you into the house we can take a look at it," said Wes.

She shook her head, not wanting to move anywhere, ever. She peeked up at her friends, who were standing around her, observing with concern in their eyes.

"Give me a minute," she said. "I just need some space." Wes and Bea went off the ice but Chloe stood quietly nearby.

The shooting pain was gradually replaced with a sharp ache that appeared to be sticking around for the long haul. Lindsay noticed for the first time since she'd fallen that her legs and backside were freezing where they touched the ice. She would need to stand soon, but it was the last thing she wanted to do.

"Chloe," she said weakly. "Will you help me up?"

Chloe walked over to her. She'd removed her skates and stood solidly in her boots. "Alright. I'm going to grab you beneath the arms, but if you need me to stop, let me know."

Lindsay gave a smidgen of a nod, and Chloe reached under her arms. The pain of moving was almost unbearable, but the alternative was to slowly freeze to the surface of the pond. Once Lindsay was standing, Chloe took her elbow and helped her into the cabin. Lindsay sat on the edge of the couch with her head down and her eyes closed, cradling her arm.

She focused on the smell of wood smoke and the sound of the pendulum clock on the antique sideboard. Nobody spoke.

"Will someone please tell me if it's broken?" she asked. "I can't look."

She gingerly pulled back the sleeve of her jacket and the layers beneath it as Bea approached her. Bea stifled a gasp then said, "It's broken."

"Is it really that bad?" Lindsay asked.

Bea hesitated. "It doesn't look good."

This was a disaster. Aside from the pain that was running through her hand and the length of her right arm, Lindsay wasn't going to be able to do everything she absolutely needed to do in order to have any chance at keeping her inn going. She held back her tears, not sure if they were coming because of the pain she'd endured and was yet to come or because she had just met her doom in a most unexpected place and time. How would she run the inn with a broken wrist?

When she was ready to go to the hospital, Arthur helped her up and guided her to Old Blue. She climbed into the passenger seat and Chloe, who had volunteered to take her, drove them down the road slowly and carefully so as not to jostle her injured friend.

"We're almost there," Chloe informed her.

Lindsay had her eyes closed again, and was trying to stay in the moment. If she thought about what was ahead of her, she started to panic. It was going to have to be one step at a time from here on out.

They pulled into the emergency room parking lot and checked in at the front desk. It was boiling in the waiting room. Chloe helped Lindsay take off her coat. It took a painful ten minutes. Just as she broke completely free from her sweltering prison, a nurse checked them in.

"Lindsay?" she said. "I'm so sorry this happened. Grace was just in this morning. She'll be able to take care of you when you get home." Lindsay nodded and shuffled down the hallway into an examining room.

The nurse asked some questions then left them to wait. What happened next was a blur of nurses, doctors, and technicians coming in and out for more questions, poking, prodding, and, worst of all, setting the bone.

"Good news," the doctor said. Lindsay doubted it. "It looks like we were able to get the bone nearly back into place. You most likely won't need surgery."

She supposed that was good news. "How long until I get my cast off?" she asked.

"That'll be up to the orthopedist, but my rough estimate would be six weeks. You should try to do as little as possible with that hand while it's healing."

As little as possible for six weeks? Everything she had done in one single week, every chore, every errand, every tweak of the wrist and heft of the arm ran through her mind. This was all so unbelievable she didn't know whether she should laugh or cry.

By the time she was back home with an appointment to get a hard cast put on and a prescription for some painkillers, she was exhausted, both physically and emotionally. Grace went into full-scale nursing mode, installing Lindsay in bed with pillows propped up all around her.

Grandma got to work right away as well, whipping up a batch of chicken noodle soup with meat that tasted like it'd come from a whole bird that had been roasting all day. Lindsay ate it gratefully.

Grace and Grandma bustled in and out of the room, delivering and taking away ice packs, books, food, and drinks. At the rare moment when they were both by her side, Lindsay asked, "What am I going to do?"

"What do ya mean?" Grandma asked. "You're going to heal up and we're going to take care of you. No offense, but when you've been around as long as I have you know that this is nothing in the scheme of things."

"I really appreciate that, but those guys are going to be here for another two weeks, and I can't do anything."

"You can do some stuff, but in the meantime, I'll take over here when Grace is at work. It'll be fine and dandy."

"What if it snows again? No one else knows how to work the snow blower. And you can't go down those basement steps, Grandma." Lindsay fixed her with a stern glance, which Grandma waved away.

"Who says I can't?"

"I do. They're barely safe for Grace and me. If

you fall down them, you'll end up with much worse than a broken wrist. I don't want you putting yourself at risk."

"Alright, I get it. Geeze...a woman asks one question...It's like trying to negotiate with an obstinate bookie around here with you two."

Grace gave Grandma her own sideways glance then chimed in. "Grandma's right, about the part where we can help you anyway. We can do this. I'll do the laundry and any other basement stuff when I'm home, and Grandma can do the cooking and cleaning when I'm gone. We'll be unstoppable."

Lindsay wasn't so sure. "I don't feel like it's fair of me to ask this of you two."

"Well, good thing you're not asking then," said Grandma. "We're telling you what we're gonna do."

Lindsay leaned back on her pillows and closed her eyes. She felt muzzy and drowsy and wanted to fall into a forgetful sleep, the kind that had been eluding her all week. "Thank you, both of you. Let's talk about it again tomorrow." She fell asleep.

Early next morning, so early that it was still dark outside, perturbation popped Lindsay upright with a start as if she'd been poked through the mattress with a needle between the shoulder blades. Her wrist throbbed and she groaned as she sat up taller. She stared down the armoire and it stared back. Picking up her phone with her left hand, she balanced it on her leg and pecked away a text.

You can come by to help, but just until we get everything sorted out.

Before she could send another one taking it back, she flung her phone across the bed. It slipped to the edge, teetered there, and fell to the floor with a thud.

Chapter Thirteen

In Which Grandma Loses Her Festive Spirit

Lindsay was in the kitchen trying to learn to cook with one full hand and a hand with only fingers. So far she'd concluded that it was going to be next to impossible to chop anything, but if someone got her started she could stir, pour, and take things out of the oven. It wasn't ideal, but if she planned their menus in advance, she could ask Grace to do the chopping when she was home.

"What are you doing in here?" Grandma had just walked in the back door, followed by Bea.

"Hey guys," said Lindsay. She explained her mission, and Grandma wasn't having any of it, adopting the air of a woman prepared to stage an uprising if such a thing proved necessary.

"You're supposed to be resting. How will your wrist ever heal if you're scooting around the kitchen at all hours? Vamoose!"

"I need to be of some use."

"And you will be, later, not less than 24 runkling hours after breaking your wrist."

Bea set a casserole and a cherry pie on the table.

"You didn't have to do that," said Lindsay.

"I wanted to though. My mom heard what happened and whipped up a couple things."

"That's so sweet. How's she doing?"

"She's really slipping lately. Dad's had to stick by her more and more. It's been a bit of challenge, getting the farm work done, but Harvey's been coming by quite a bit."

"He's amazing. How does he do it?"

"He's always been one to have a hundred different irons in the fire. I don't think he'd have it any other way."

"Well that's good to hear. Maybe we shouldn't tell him about my wrist for a couple of days."

Bea looked apologetic. "I already told him when he came by this morning."

"It's fine. I'm sure he won't…

There was knock at the door. Grandma ran to answer it. It was Harvey. "Why hello," Grandma said. "Your whole family's stopping by today."

Harvey stomped the snow off his boots and came inside. "Oh, hey Bea. I see you already brought some food over."

"How could you tell it was from me?" Bea asked.

"I recognize Mom's casserole dish. How're you feeling?" he asked Lindsay, walking over to her and giving her a big hug. She leaned her head into his soft flannel warmth, tempted to stay there a while. Two sets of eyes-friendly and grandma-ly-ones bore into her back though, so she backed up after an appropriately short interval for two people who were just platonic friends and would never be any more than that and why would anyone ever think otherwise?

"Why, look at that," said Grandma. "You two are standing under the mistletoe. What are the chances?"

Lindsay scanned the kitchen ceiling and considered that the odds were pretty good. In fact, Grandma was standing under a clump of the stuff herself at the moment. Bea would be too, if she scooted over about a foot.

"I'm doing alright," said Lindsay, ignoring Grandma's comment and answering Harvey's question. "The medicine is helping with the pain. It's more frustrating than anything."

"I bet," he said. "You're busy around here, but you'll just have to rely on us to help you for a while."

Lindsay shook her head. "I appreciate your thoughtfulness, both you and Grace, but I know you have so much on your plates. Between Grace, Grandma, and me, we've got everything under control. All this food is more than enough help." Her table was covered with food now. Harvey had made muffins and a loaf of bread too.

He noticed Lindsay looking at it and said, "Maddie wanted me to let you know that the glaze on that bread was made with an egg that was cracked with only one hand."

"Tell her thank you for me. I'm very impressed." Lindsay threw a hand to her mouth and gasped.

"What is it?"

"I won't be able to do the holiday bake-off now. It's in three days. Maddie's going to be so disappointed."

"She'll be fine. We can all go together and watch Tom and Mrs. Martel go head to head."

Lindsay nodded sadly. She knew Harvey was just being polite, which was sweet but…"What if Maddie and I teamed up?"

"I love it. Is that allowed?"

"I'm not sure. I'll check with Emma today. I doubt there are official regulations. If she says it's alright, Maddie can be the hands of the operation. We'll need a practice run, but do you think she'd want to do it?"

"I think she'll be beside herself with excitement."

"Perfect. I'll let you know if I get the go-ahead from Emma." Lindsay couldn't believe she hadn't thought of this before. It would've been a great idea with or without her broken wrist. There it was: a silver lining.

"Well, I better run. It's going to be tough not to tell Maddie about your scheme. I can't wait to see her face if she gets to be a contestant. She's been talking about watching you all week. It's great to see you looking so good. I was really worried when I heard the news." He hugged her again before heading out the door.

Bea followed soon after. When they had gone, Grandma said, "Did you hear that? He said you were looking good. Now there's a man who knows how to treat a woman."

"Sorry, who are we talking about?"

"Don't play coy with me. That Harvey Delcroix is the bee's knees."

Lindsay couldn't help but chuckle. She opened the fridge and Grandma slid the casserole and soup inside. "He's a great guy," Lindsay agreed.

Grandma scoffed. "Great? He's a saint. And I'll eat this oven mitt if he's not your secret admirer."

Lindsay took the mitt from her hand and put it back on the tree. "I'm just not sure…"

"What aren't you sure about?"

"I'm still married, remember?"

"Married schmaried. Doesn't mean much if he's never around. Speaking of he who shall remain nameless, have you heard from him?"

"Actually…"

Grandma turned from the sink and looked her granddaughter in the eye. "What happened?"

"I texted Steve early this morning and told him he could come around and help with some things."

"Is that what you really want? Despite all appearances, I do realize that I'm an old lady, but I'm telling you, I can take over here for a while."

"I know you can Grandma, it isn't about that. It's just…I think I need to be around him one last time before I make a final decision. And besides, it would be nice to have some extra help around here."

"So you're thinking about taking him back?" Her grandma's expression slid from annoyance to despair.

"I'm not sure what to think. I'm wondering how much I contributed to what happened between us."

Grandma scoffed but Lindsay continued. "It's just that I haven't seen him at all since he left. It's sort of a way to get clarity and get some help at the same time. I know it doesn't make sense, but…"

"No. It doesn't," said Grandma. Lindsay had never seen her so sour faced and angry. "I'm sorry, but I can't understand it. It's not that I haven't tried to see it from your perspective, but what he's put you through-you and Betsy and me too, for that matter-it's not right."

A knock at the door interrupted their discussion. Lindsay headed over to greet another visitor. It was Steve, with a big smile on his face, and he couldn't have come at a more inopportune moment.

"I got your text this morning," he said as she let him into the kitchen. "Hi Grandma Vivian."

"Hello there," she said, doing her best to appear friendly towards him. It looked painful.

"What happened to your arm?" he asked, noticing Lindsay's cast.

"I broke my wrist skating yesterday," she explained.

"Well this is going to make my surprise even better," he said. Lindsay was still taken aback at how normal he seemed, like it was natural that he would come back into her life and everything would go back to the way it had been before. He was taking it for granted that all was forgiven, and it made Lindsay uncomfortable.

"A surprise?" she asked, not sure that she liked where this was going, and fully aware that he'd expressed no concern about her injury.

"Yeah. It's in the garage. Come on out."

Lindsay slipped on her boots and followed him outside, being extra careful on the steps. He headed to the back of the garage where she kept the snow blower. In place of the old model was a shiny new one. In fact, it was the very one that she'd passed up because it was way out of her price range. The vision was one that should've inspired elation, but she felt flat instead.

"So," he said, "what to do you think?"

"It's really nice. Did you bring it over for the day?" It was supposed to snow that night. Maybe he was thinking of using it tomorrow morning.

"It's for you to keep here. I took the old one. We can swap. My driveway's tiny anyway."

It was a vast improvement on what sat there before, but she wished he would've asked before he made the switch. She couldn't bring herself to say so though. Instead, she said, "Oh. Alright."

"I thought you'd be happy. That old snow blower was always such a pain." He furrowed his brow.

She tried to brighten her tone. "I am. It's great.

Thanks."

"I can take it back if you don't want it."

"No. Like I said, it's great. I have a lot going on right now, sorry."

"No problem." His forehead smoothed and he grinned. "I'm planning on coming over every other evening. You can tell me what to do."

That often? This wasn't what Lindsay had in mind. She thought she'd call him a few times when she needed help and then they could discuss what they were going to do. How could she tell him that? He seemed ready to jump right back in where they left off. She'd have to be clearer about what she had in mind, but she was nervous about how he would take it. In the past she would start out trying to say one thing, and he'd turn it into something else by the time they were finished.

"Sounds good," she said. She could ask him to stop coming around any time.

"Well, I'm here now. Is there something that needs doing?"

Lindsay considered. "Sure. Could you rake the snow off the roof?"

"Of course." Steve walked straight to where the roof rake was hung up in the garage and grabbed it off the wall. "Anything else?"

"I don't think so."

"Alright, let me know." He strolled out, leaving Lindsay to wonder what she had done, and how difficult it would be to take it back.

Chapter Fourteen

In Which Life is What You Bake It

"Welcome to the fortieth annual Emma's Cafe Holiday Bake-Off." Emma stood before a packed diner in her festive red and black checkered uniform. Half the town was in attendance, not to mention the newcomers who had been creating such a stir: Brian, Moose, and Hook. Everyone cheered as their hostess introduced the contestants. "On the left we have Janine Martel with her Christmas mille-feuille."

Linsday raised her eyebrows. Mille-feuille was complicated. So many things could go wrong. Mrs. Martel would be making her puff pastry from scratch, of course, something that Lindsay often eschewed in favor of the store bought variety. (Her guests didn't seem to know the difference.) Thin sheets of pastry would be alternated with crème patissiere, a custard that needed to be cooled until it reached a perfect thickness or it would ooze from the between the layers.

Mrs. Martel waved to her family. She hadn't been in the competition for ages; her grandchildren had never seen her compete. The youngest one, who couldn't have been older than three pointed, saying "That's Grandma!" and everyone chuckled.

The grocery maven had grumbled when she heard that a team of two would be competing in the bake-off. When she found out that one of the members was nine and the other had a broken wrist, however, she backed down and the preparations for the contest proceeded without further protestations.

Emma continued. "Front and center we have Lindsay Thompson and Madison Delcroix with their buche de Noel. For those who aren't aware, this is a historical moment; Maddie is the youngest competitor ever." The crowd went wild.

Grandma yelled, "Go get 'em ladies!"

Lindsay reached over to grab Maddie's hand, fearing she'd be nervous. She needn't have worried. Maddie slipped away and ran around the counter, curtseying and beaming before hurrying back to her partner's side.

Everyone from the Demeter Society was there to cheer them on as well, plus Harvey, James, Arthur, and Wes. Betsy was up and about serving drinks and food. She'd stayed on at Emma's part-time after Chloe hired her. She claimed it was only until Emma found a replacement, but Emma wasn't looking very hard and Betsy never asked about it. It was likely they'd carry on with the arrangement for a good long time.

"And on the far right, we have newcomer Tom

Chaudeux, who is making a valiant attempt to recreate my coconut diner cake," said Emma with a dubious raise of the eyebrows. The crowd clapped for him as well. "I must say, making one of my own recipes is bold move, but he's been hanging around here long enough that he must think he's picked up enough tips to make it happen."

It was true. Tom was mostly retired from farming, aside from his little Christmas tree farm, and he loved nothing more than to sit on the bench in front of Emma's spinning tall tales with whoever would join him. He must have been sneaking into the kitchen every now and then as well. Lindsay couldn't blame him. Emma and her husband Ernie were the best chefs in town. They had a wealth of experience, having run the cafe for ages, and the fact that they put copious amounts of butter in just about everything didn't hurt either.

"Alright bakers, the clock starts now. You have two hours to complete your holiday confection and present it to the judges."

The judges were the same every year, and they varied in their exactitude. Connie, the former head librarian, was the toughest. She wouldn't let a soggy crust or a flat meringue pass without comment. Chloe's mom Tammi was easy. She gushed about everything. Ernie, who did most of the cooking at the café, was usually the middle of the road judge, but he and Maddie were buddies. Maybe that would sway his determination in their favor.

In fact, most of the crowd had their eyes on

Maddie and she knew it. Instead of making her nervous, though, she was in top form, not waiting for Lindsay to tell her what to do to get started. She cracked three eggs into a bowl with one hand in quick succession. "Did you see that?" she called to her dad. "I did it!"

"You're a natural," he said. "Keep up the good work."

Lindsay plugged in the beaters and Maddie whisked the eggs until they were lemon colored and smooth, only splattering herself and Lindsay a little bit. "I'm even better than when we practiced."

Maddie took over entirely, reading the recipe and only checking with Lindsay to make sure her measurements were right. Lindsay couldn't believe it and apparently neither could Harvey. He may have shed a tear or two during the proceedings, but it was hard to be sure from where Lindsay was standing.

Maddie tipped the cake batter into a prepared pan, and Lindsay slid it into the oven. They didn't have long to wait. When they pulled the baked cake out, Lindsay held her breath. This was going to be the tricky part. She could probably wiggle it out of the pan, but Maddie was going to have to roll it up. When they'd practiced at the inn, the cake had broken and cracked. Her junior baker had been beside herself, but Lindsay assured her that it had just been slightly over-baked. They'd cut their baking time today and hope for a better result.

Lindsay flipped the pan onto a towel with her good hand. The cake came out perfectly golden and smooth. Alright, this was the moment of truth. Maddie gently slid her hands under the towel and began to roll.

"It's working!" she said. "Look, it's working!"

When she got to the end, they examined it from the side. There wasn't a single crack in sight.

"Well done," said Lindsay. "You did it."

Maddie shimmied behind the table then ran over to give her dad a hug before coming back to finish the job. They needed to make the filling next. Maddie poured the whipping cream, sugar, and coffee crystals into a big bowl and flipped on the mixer. The cream flew across the room, splattering the people watching nearby as well as all four contestants. The young baker flipped off the switch, said "Sorry guys," and went back to mixing. This time most of the cream stayed in the bowl, but Lindsay dabbed a bit off her nose and cheeks and would find some in her hair when she showered later that evening.

The cake roll was stuffed with whipped cream and topped with rich chocolate frosting, which had come together beautifully. Lindsay and Maddie were just sifting powdered sugar on top of their perfectly formed log when Emma announced that they had five minutes remaining.

Maddie jumped up and down, pumping her arms. "We did it. We did it. We did it." Her apron was coated with every ingredient they'd used and most of her hair had slipped out of her ponytail.

Mrs. Martel was just finishing up as well. Her mille-feuille were pristine. They were stuffed with cherries and she'd piped green pistachio custard between the layers. Tom's coconut cake was complete as well. If she hadn't known it was his, Lindsay would've mistaken it for Emma's. He'd made two round cakes and frosted them with a coconut buttercream. The frosting was evenly toasted all around. It was going to be a tight competition.

Maddie tiptoed over to Mrs. Martel's table and asked if she could have a cherry dipped in custard and of course she received not one but two. She popped them in her mouth and darted back to Lindsay's side just as Emma announced, "Bakers, your time is up. Please step away from your desserts so they can be presented to the judges."

Maddie sprinted over to sit next to her grandparents, who were squished into a booth with her dad, James, and Bea. The young baker chatted excitedly about how much fun she'd had and what she wanted to make at next year's competition. She sipped her grandma's chocolate malt, not noticing when it was announced that she and Lindsay had won.

Lindsay ran over and told her the good news.

"What?" Maddie said. "We won? No way."

"Yes way," said James. "Go up there and collect your prize."

"There's a prize?"

Maddie jumped up and made her way over to Emma, who handed her a basket of cookies. Maddie held the trophy above her head triumphantly while Lindsay looked on, smiling with pride at her little friend. "Come on," said Maddie, waving her partner to stand beside her. "You need to hold it too."

Lindsay joined her and everyone clapped and cheered.

"We need to take a picture so we can put you up on the hall of fame," said Emma.

"We get to be in the hall of fame?" Maddie asked.

"You bet. You're the winners."

Maddie struck a pose and Emma snapped a photo of the winning team. Maddie checked it over and nodded her approval then she and Lindsay headed over to the wall to admire the pictures of previous years' winners.

"There's my mom," Maddie said, pointing to a photo of a beautiful blonde woman posing in front of an elaborate éclair. It was from Leah's last year in the competition. She'd just discovered she was sick. "Was I there when she won?"

"You were. You would've been two then. You ran around between the tables and then fell asleep in your dad's lap."

Maddie nodded her head thoughtfully. She was approached by Mrs. Martel and Tom, who shook her hand in congratulations.

Lindsay looked over the wall of fame one last time before joining her friends and family. They enjoyed mille-feuille, buche de Noel, and the second best coconut cake ever tasted at Emma's Café.

When the action had died down and people were starting to leave, Harvey invited Lindsay to come back to his house for an extension on the celebration. Grace, who had overheard him and picked up on Lindsay's hesitation said, "Go. We'll be fine."

"Thanks," said Lindsay, who really had wanted to spend a bit more time celebrating with her teammate.

Lindsay and Maddie said goodbye to their remaining supporters and Lindsay followed the Delcroix family home. Maddie jumped out of the truck the second they arrived and shouted a victory chant all the way inside. They made their way into the living room, where the young champion slumped into a plush armchair. It was only seven o'clock, but she was starting to look glassy-eyed.

"I'm going into the basement to play," she said, yawning. James followed her downstairs, leaving Lindsay and Harvey alone on the couch.

Big day for you guys," said Harvey. "I clearly don't need to tell you this, but you've made Maddie's month."

Lindsay laughed. "She certainly doesn't hold her feelings inside. I had a great time too. Maddie was amazing. I think I may have just created some fierce competition for my future self."

"There's no doubt she'll be back. You've been such a special person in her life, mine too." Harvey took Lindsay's hands in his. She felt herself being drawn to him and fought to find a way to drop anchor before she could drift so close that there would be no turning back. Was he about to kiss her? It appeared that he was. He leaned in and she put her hands on

AMANDA SCHWANTES

his cheeks to stop him. Their foreheads bumped and he smiled. He was so sweet, but that's why Lindsay needed to be honest with him. She reluctantly backed away.

"I need to talk to you about something," she said.

"I'm sorry. I shouldn't have…"

"No. I'm sorry. I was starting to get a feeling that something was happening between us, with the presents and everything, and I should've spoken up sooner."

"Presents?" He scrunched his eyebrows together. Apparently he wasn't her secret Santa.

"You haven't been leaving me presents on my back doorstep?"

"I wish I'd thought of it, but no, it's not me."

Well, this was awkward. Now Lindsay was the one with the scrunchy face. "Okay, well, I mean…" How could she explain something that she had barely figured out for herself? "What I'm trying to say is that I love your family, and…"

"We love you too," Harvey interrupted.

"But the thing is, this situation is really complicated. You're, well, you're you and you have your kids, and I wouldn't want to take any kind of a place like that in their lives, or in your life, until I was sure that it was the right thing."

Harvey nodded as if he understood. He also knew that she was still in a very odd place with Steve. He didn't know just how odd though, and she owed it to him to be honest.

"Steve is coming back to help out at the inn."

"Oh," he said, his face unreadable. He shifted away from her.

"I haven't seen him since this summer, so I'm considering it an opportunity to talk to him and figure out what I want going forward. What's best for me."

Harvey sighed, looking up and away from her for a moment, and Lindsay's heart raced. What was he thinking? Was he hurt? Disappointed? This was exactly what Lindsay had feared. When Harvey finally spoke, he said, "I'm sorry. I got carried away with the excitement of the day. We should take a little space from each other while you're figuring this out. I'll just muddle things for you, and I don't want anyone to get hurt."

Did he mean him, his kids, or Lindsay herself? Probably all three, and he was right. He didn't clarify and she didn't dare ask him to. She wanted to curl up into a ball and be transported back to her house. Instead, she sat there stiffly, finally saying, "I'm going to head out. I'd like to say goodbye to Maddie, if that's alright."

"Of course it is," Harvey said, the sadness on his face reflecting the hollow ache that Lindsay felt in the pit of her stomach.

She went into the basement, where the kids were fiddling with a science kit at a card table.

"Great job today," Lindsay told her partner.

"You too," said Maddie, running over to Lindsay and giving her a big hug. "Can we do it again next year?"

"You bet."

"Even if your wrist isn't broken?"

"It better not be!" Lindsay laughed. "But whether it is or not, we'll be a team."

"Yes!"

"Goodnight guys, be good for your dad."

"We will." Maddie had reinstated her wicked grin.

"She's still thinking about going for coal from Santa, but I don't think she can be bad if she tries," said James.

"I can too!"

"I'll believe it when I see it."

"Dad!"

"Goodnight you two," Lindsay said again. She clomped upstairs, passing Harvey on his way down. They gave each other a half-hearted smile, and Lindsay showed herself out. Hiding her chin in her jacket and pulling her hat down tight against the biting cold, she started up her car and drove away.

Chapter Fifteen

In Which Yuletide Carols are Sung By a Choir

"We're on a roll," said Grace, going over her Christmas activity checklist. "I wouldn't be surprised if we complete the entire list for the first time."

"Wow. Really?" Linsday asked, feigning enthusiasm.

Lindsay sat down at the table and slid the list in front of her. Christmas tree acquired? Check. Snowball fight? Check. Tree decorated? Check. Holiday Bake-off? Check. Halls decked? Big check. Kiss under the mistletoe? Check. Lindsay looked up and Grace blushed. Alright, Grace gets the check for that one. Lindsay, not so much.

Lindsay cringed when she thought about what had happened between her and Harvey the night before. It could've gone so much differently if she hadn't said anything about Steve, but she wouldn't have felt good about it today.

Harvey was a good friend, and he didn't deserve all this capitulation on her part. Lindsay would keep her distance until she was crystal clear on where her life was headed. He'd probably have moved on by then, but that was a chance she'd have to take. Lindsay slouched in her chair.

Grace got up and pulled the cutting board out of the cupboard. She pushed around the recipe books in the cabinet above the stove, looking for something. "Where's the recipe box?"

"Mom took it to Florida."

"But it had all of our family recipes in it."

"I have them too; we copied them together before she left." Lindsay got up and pulled out a battered yellow folder. Printouts, note cards, and papers tumbled out of its ripped side. "Oops, sorry. It gets a lot of use."

"This is a mess. You need a recipe box."

"I'll put it on my list to Santa." Lindsay found the stir fry recipe and slid it onto the counter.

Grace read it over. She chopped veggies and bagged them before putting them in the fridge. "Are you still coming caroling tonight?"

Lindsay had completely forgotten. They were supposed to be going with the Demeter Society ladies.

"Grandma and the hunters are coming along too," Grace added. "Hey, that would make a good band name: Grandma and the Sasquatch Hunters."

They both laughed and Lindsay said, "Yes. I'll be there. I can't wait."

"Me neither," said Grace, chopping some broccoli. "I can't believe you guys never went caroling before. Wait until everyone hears your voice again."

Lindsay stood up and nabbed a floret of broccoli from the board with her good hand, avoiding Grace's knife. "I'm not that great at singing."

"Umm...yes you are. You have a degree in singing."

"I have a degree in music theory."

"At any rate, you never sing any more."

"Sure I do..." But when Lindsay considered it some more, she supposed she really hadn't sung in a long time. Maybe she'd be rusty. She'd been interested in joining the choir at Saint Mary of the Snows, but Steve had said...it would take up too much of her time. Huh. Apparently he'd said that a lot.

"Don't you have to get to work?" Lindsay asked. It was getting late.

"Not yet..." Grace checked the clock. It was quarter to nine. "Yikes. Where did the time go? I should've left five minutes ago." She shoved the rest of the vegetables into bags and threw on her coat before racing to her car.

Lindsay stocked the fridge with the chopped veggies then spent the morning vacuuming with one hand, dusting with one hand, and pecking response emails to prospective guests who had questions about the inn. She could do more than she'd expected with a broken wrist, but everything took her four times as long as it usually did.

Lindsay hadn't seen Grandma all morning. She

must've left even earlier than the hunters, who had headed out at the break of dawn. She and Lindsay hadn't talked much since Steve had come back, and things had been chilly between them. Was Grandma avoiding her?

Vivian appeared in the kitchen at lunchtime with a cute new pixie cut and smile wrinkles around her eyes. "I hope you weren't looking for me. I stopped back at my apartment to make sure that everything was in order. Hadn't seen my friends in a while, you know."

"How's everyone doing back there?"

Grandma threw up her hands dramatically. "Oh boy, the usual. It's nothing but drama, drama, drama with some of those people."

Lindsay could imagine that somehow. "Do you want something to drink? An eggnog?"

"If that's your peculiar way of pronouncing cherry bounce, then yes, I'll take one."

Lindsay poured a glass of dark pink liqueur over ice, and Grandma reluctantly accepted it. "I shouldn't," she said, "but I will." She took a big gulp and inspected Grace's Christmas list. "I see someone else has been kissing under the mistletoe."

"Someone else?"

"Hey, *I'm* an unencumbered woman. If I happen to end up beneath the mistletoe with a handsome gent, I'll take the opportunity." She sipped her drink for emphasis. "Will Betsy be caroling tonight?"

"I'm not sure. I imagine she will."

"When's that girl going to tell people she's

pregnant?"

"Why are you saying that?"

"Oh please, don't look so surprised, unless you really don't know. James asked for a bowl full of pickles at the bake-off. When Betsy dropped them off she looked as green as those cukes. She tossed them on the table and ran into the bathroom faster than a knife fight in a phone booth."

"Okay. You're right, she's pregnant. But no, she hasn't told many people. She's working up to it."

"I'm not going to blab, but I think there may have been other folks at the café who observed her peculiar behavior as well, if you take my meaning."

"Sarah?"

Grandma gave a single nod and took another sip of her cocktail. Was she just using that drink for emphasis? It was kind of a neat trick. "Anyway, I gotta run. Lunch date with Esther. I'll be back for caroling. We have to go to the holiday parade afterwards." She jabbed an item on the list.

Sure enough, holiday parade was number six. Were these in any particular order? Huh...Number one was Christmas Monkey. Lindsay hadn't noticed that before. "What's Christmas Monkey?" she asked.

"Darned if I know. See ya fruitcake." Grandma swung a pearl studded scarf around her neck and swept out the door.

At dinner time, Lindsay pulled together a beautiful stir fry with the help of her sister's chopped veggies. Grace was home just in time to eat, and the hunters had returned as well. They were all fired up about more footprints they'd found out near Tom's place that were identical to the ones on Lindsay's property.

"When we were out there, I could feel someone watchin' us, all sneaky-like," said Hook. "I don't know guys; the closer we get the more elusive he seems."

Brian wouldn't be discouraged. "Think of how far we've come in only nine days. Besides, we're nearly surrounded by water here. We've got him cornered. This isn't like the wilds of Montana or Wyoming. The only way to escape is south, and there's nothing but farm fields and cities that way. No, this is our shot."

"Can they swim?" Grace asked between bites.

All three men looked at each other, unsure. "I'm gonna say yes," said Moose. "I don't see why not." The other two nodded and continued eating in silence.

"Could they swim far?" She pressed. "Yes, we're surrounded by water, but what if they could swim across the bay?"

Moose and Hook looked to their leader, who shook his head. "They're specialized to survive in the wilderness; they can't swim long distances too."

"It makes sense though, doesn't it?" said Moose. "Maybe that's why they're so elusive. They could swim out into the lake at night and it would be like they disappeared. No one would suspect it." He took another bite and his eyes widened. "Or even, oh wow, what about this? Maybe they have some kind of huge lung capacity, or gills even. That way they could disappear underwater during the day too."

Brian looked annoyed. "Let's operate under the assumption that he won't escape via an aquatic route for the time being."

"You can just hang onto it as a working hypothesis," said Grace. Moose and Hook nodded in appreciation.

Brian sighed and changed the subject. "We're ready and raring to go for caroling tonight. We'll have to do some vocal warm-ups inside first though. It's nippy out there, does a number on the old vocal chords."

"You three sing?" Lindsay asked.

"Do we? Hit it boys. One, two, three." The three men broke into a bouncy rendition of *It's Beginning to Look a Lot Like Christmas* in three part harmony.

Grace and Lindsay's jaws dropped in unison.

"You should make a record," said Grace, when they had finished. They waved her compliment away. "I mean it. You're incredible. We already have a band name for you. It'll work if you let Grandma Vivian join."

"I thought she was your mother," said Brian.

Grace put her hand to her mouth. She hadn't meant to expose Grandma's ruse. Brian laughed. "I was onto her from the start."

"Onto who?" Grandma stomped her feet in the entrance.

"You have to hear these guys sing," said Grace. "They're amazing."

"Really? I wouldn't have taken you three for

travelling troubadours."

"We don't advertise it, but when we're out hunting we end up with a lot of time on our hands. We taught ourselves from videos. It passes the time and surprises people. The looks on your faces...sorry, but it just never gets old."

"Well let's get going then," said Grandma, leaving on her coat. "I've gotta hear this."

They met the rest of the Demeter Society at Chloe's house to serenade her unsuspecting neighbors. The first house they visited was right next door. The man who answered always struck Lindsay as reminiscent of Mister Rodgers in both demeanor and dress. Tonight he wore a hunter green cardigan and khaki slacks.

"Well what do we have here?" he asked.

The whole group broke into song, beginning with *We Wish You a Merry Christmas*. The man beamed, clasping his hands together as if he couldn't contain his pleasure at being serenaded. Grandma sang the loudest and most joyfully, coming across somewhat akin to an exuberant foghorn. The combined effect of all their voices together was glorious.

The hunters followed up with *Silent Night* and Lindsay joined in as the soprano. She got goose bumps, having forgotten how it felt to raise her voice in a group that became so much more than the sum of its parts.

The rest of the houses went the same way. They all sang one song together, sometimes joined by the friendly neighbors. Afterwards, the quartet sang another song or two. Everyone was thrilled to be serenaded and astonished when the quartet broke into song. The singers were plied with cider, cocoa, and candy canes and invited inside to warm up, an offer they gratefully accepted.

They sang themselves all the way to Main Street, where the streetlights were decorated with tinsel shaped as bells, trees, and stars. The shops were decked out for the season as well. A rocking horse, jack-in-the-box, and toy train graced the window of the antique shop. White lights encircled the snow covered spruce outside the church. Even the mechanic's was bedazzled with strings of lights in the windows and a glittering snowman at the entrance.

The townsfolk lined the road, some with kids on their shoulders, some holding bags in anticipation of collecting the candy that would be tossed from the floats. The carolers found Arthur and Wes along the route and sidled up next to them. The two men were treated to a sample of their tunes, and everyone nearby turned to listen.

When they had finished singing, Lindsay scanned the crowd. Were Harvey, James, and Maddie here? They were sure to be, unless they were out of town. They hadn't missed the holiday parade in all the years Lindsay had known them. Her heart sank at the thought of seeing Harvey and being the giver and recipient of another forced and melancholy grin.

Sure enough, there they were, on the other side of the road and down the way a bit. Maybe they hadn't seen her yet. At that moment, Maddie pointed in

Lindsay's direction and hopped up and down. Lindsay waved, told her friends she'd be right back, hopped off the curb, and walked across the street for a quick hello.

She slowed her steps as she got closer, ostensibly admiring the festive trappings of Main Street but actually rehearsing what she'd say when she reached them. Would a casual "hey" be alright? She didn't want to sound flippant. "Hello there" might be acceptable, but she'd never say that, normally. What would she normally say? Something like, "I'm sorry I made everything so awkward, and I've wanted to crawl under a rock ever since you tried to kiss me even though I wish you'd do it again?" Yikes.

"Hey-ho guys." That? That was what she had ended up going with after all that deliberation? It was pitiful, but there is was, and there it would remain.

"Hey Lindsay," said James. "You have a really good voice."

"Oh. Thanks," she said, taken aback. She didn't realize they would've been able to hear her from all the way over here.

Maddie had already come over to hug her and was pressing her face into Lindsay's parka. "You were great. You're a baker and a singer. Can you teach me to sing too?"

"Of course. We can be singing bakers together."

Maddie's mouth formed into an "o" of shock at the brilliant idea. "Who taught you to sing? It sure wasn't Grandma Vivian."

Lindsay laughed. "How could you tell?"

Maddie pursed her lips together and glanced at her dad before whispering, "She sings really loud, but it's not really...well, you know." She shrugged.

"I do know," Lindsay whispered. "Grandma loves to sing, and that's the most important part, but I sang in the church choir and at school too. I had a really special music teacher who's not there any more. I hear the new one is really good too though."

Harvey listened in, watching his kids while avoiding catching Lindsay's eye. She should be the one to break the ice. "Looks like a big turn-out this year for the parade," she said to Harvey. Maybe she should've added another "hey-ho" for good measure.

"They always do a nice job with it," he replied, nodding his head and looking around. He turned his bright hazel eyes to hers and gave her a smile that, contrary to her expectations, wasn't rueful at all. If anything, Lindsay detected a confidence that would classify it as hopeful. Was he still hanging on for a Christmas miracle? She didn't know whether to be sorry or elated.

She smiled back and hoped it looked somewhere in between those two extremes. "I hate to run so soon," she said, "but my friends are waiting for me over there, and it looks like the parade is about to start. You guys have fun."

"Bye Lindsay," the kids called, and she waved over her shoulder as she rejoined the carolers.

The parade kicked off with Roy, Sarah's husband and the town board president, gliding by in the passenger seat of his antique car. He gave a regal wave and nodded officially to his wife and his son Arthur as he passed. The volunteer firefighters came by next. They had gone all out this year. A light-up reindeer flew off the end of their ladder, over the head of the driver. Glowing candy canes crisscrossed the windows, and blue and green lights zigzagged across its side.

Chloe nudged Lindsay and pointed to Wes, who had gotten down on one knee in front of Bea. Lindsay gasped. His laces weren't untied this time. He reached into his coat pocket. Had a glint of sparkle shone out from between his fingers? His unsuspecting girlfriend hadn't noticed yet. She was waving to the men in the fire truck.

Wes stood and pulled two foil wrapped chocolates from his jacket. "Look what they're throwing this year," he said. "I love these crispy chocolate guys." He unwrapped the Santa and took a bite off his feet before handing the other one to Bea.

"Is he doing this to us on purpose?" Chloe asked.

Officer Anselme drove by in his squad car next. He wore a Santa hat and had eschewed his glasses. He spotted Grace and she blew him a kiss. He smiled and caught it. Oh boy, what was Lindsay in for with those two?

"Are you feeling alright, dear? You're looking rather tired," Sarah said to Betsy.

"What?" Betsy asked, snapping out of a daze. "Oh, yes. I am feeling really tired actually. Do you mind if we walk back, Chloe?"

Chloe turned to her sister. "Sure. Let's go."

"I'll join you," said Arthur, taking Chloe's arm.

"But you'll miss Santa," said Chloe.

"I'll live," Arthur chuckled.

"What a gentleman."

"I learned from the best." Arthur gave his mom a wink and Sarah smiled back.

Betsy, Chloe, and Arthur said goodbye and strolled down the road. Sarah followed them with watchful eyes as they left.

Chapter Sixteen

In Which a Holly Jolly Christmas is More Elusive Than Ever

The following day, Lindsay galumphed to the garage to face down her first challenge of the morning: attempting to use the shiny new snow blower with one hand. Would such a thing even be possible?

No matter what happened, it was sure to be a very different experience from what she was accustomed to. It had been said by others-not its owner, who didn't feel that charitable- that her old snow blower's age had given it character. Lindsay, however, argued that it was possessed. When she debated using it, when there wasn't really all that much snow, and she could just grab the shovel to get the job done if she had the time, it started up like a dream.

Then there were days like today, when mother nature dropped a foot of heavy snow and took only a short break to appreciate what she had done before throwing down another six inches for good measure. On those special days, the blower responded as if it had never run before and never would again.

Lindsay used to whistle a ditty as she opened the garage door. She'd act casual in front of the ancient machine. She knew it was illogical to think her snow blower picked up on her attitude, but it didn't hurt to Today, she edged around her car and found not only the new snow blower, but also Steve. He waved merrily, preparing to start it up.

"Morning," he said, once again acting as if this was just another day at the Thomson homestead. "You're not going to believe how this puppy runs. I bet I'll have this whole driveway done in twenty minutes."

Lindsay adjusted her features so her surprise wouldn't show. She got closer to inspect the new contraption. "It certainly looks impressive. Can you show me how it works?"

Steve waved her away. "That's alright. I know how you are with machines. Don't want this one to start breaking down too."

Excuse me? "I've been learning quite a bit. I bet you'd be surprised."

Steve must have picked up on her irritation, because he said, "Yeah, I bet I would, but you don't have to do this stuff anymore now that I'm around."

"I hear what you're saying," said Lindsay, trying to keep her temper in check. Why was it bothering her so much? He used to say things like this so often it was like a refrain, like background noise that she'd learned to tune out. Now, however, she was surprised by the flicker of anger rising in her chest. "I like to know how to do things too, and I'm quite capable when given a chance."

"Sure you are," he chuckled. He looked ready to rub the tassel on her hat. "How about next time? I need to get to work."

Lindsay took a deep breath and let it out. "Or, you could use the time to show me how it runs, and then I could..."

Brrrrrrrr. Steve started the snow blower as if he hadn't heard her and headed down the driveway, leaving behind the scent of burning gas and condescension. He'd been right about one thing; it really could throw a lot of snow. Lindsay didn't stay to watch him, preferring to head inside and start breakfast. She could come back out later, when Steve was gone, to try to shovel out the guys' trucks.

She didn't know who she would've rather faced, her husband or that cheeky old snow blower. On second thought, she did know, the possessed blower may not have cooperated with her, but at least it couldn't talk back.

Grandma sat in the kitchen sipping coffee. "What's gotten into you? You look like five miles of bad road," she said as Lindsay stomped inside.

"It's a long story."

"I bet it's not. I bet it starts with an S and ends with a –teve. I can hear him out there with his big fancy machine. He thinks he's helping, but if you ask me he's about as useful a screen door on a submarine."

Grandma looked like a woman who'd sat down with a big bowl of raspberries, and the first one she came across was a moldy one.

"This isn't funny, Grandma."

"I know it's not. I don't like that man waltzing back in here like he owns the place."

"Well, he does own it. He owns half of it, anyway. We bought it together."

"That may be, but it's been in our family for generations, and we may end up losing it when all is said and done if you don't do something about it."

Now Lindsay's hackles were raised as well. "I understand what this place means to you. It means a lot to me too. Haven't you seen me doing everything I can, practically knocking myself out every single day, so that I can keep the inn going and save my home? That's not just for me. That's for you, and Grace, and my parents, and everyone who's come before us."

Her Grandma waved her comment away, and it was all Lindsay could do not to scream with frustration. "I will not be bullied into deciding what to do with my life," she said. "You can take that or leave it."

Now it was Grandma's turn to be surprised. She softened her tone a bit, but her gaze was still steely. "I don't think I can stick around while that man continues to be a presence in this home. I'm sorry that I don't appreciate the privilege of watching someone treat my granddaughter like this."

"That's up to you. I'm going to keep doing what I need to do to figure this out."

Grandma took another sip of coffee. She pursed

her lips then said, "I'm going to gather my things. I'll eat breakfast when I get home."

She got up stiffly, and marched away. Lindsay couldn't believe this was happening. Was her grandma really going to leave? It appeared that she was. She appeared back downstairs ten minutes later. She carried her bag to the door and said formally, "We both need some space to think things through, and you need to figure out who and what you want in your life."

"That's up to you, Grandma, I'm..."

She didn't give Lindsay a chance to finish before she walked out the door.

Lindsay was devastated, but she didn't have the luxury of moping. She pulled a dozen eggs out of the fridge and cracked them into a bowl. Grandma swept back inside a moment later.

"I forgot that I'm still snowed in," she said with strained dignity.

Lindsay kept whisking her eggs. Should she ask her to stay? What could she say though? Nothing had changed. She wasn't going to promise that Steve wasn't going to come around any more. She wasn't ready to do that yet, and she didn't think she should have to. Before she could figure out what to say, the door closed behind her and Grandma was gone for good this time.

Brian, Hook, and Moose didn't ask about Grandma when they came down for breakfast. She was out and about so often that it wasn't unusual for her to be absent all day. They ate as heartily as ever while Lindsay ran out to shovel their trucks free.

Steve was gone and the driveway was otherwise completely clear of snow. Lindsay quickly realized that shoveling with one arm was going to be almost comically slow going and hoped she'd finish the job before evening fell. She had just moved her third tiny shovel full when Brian ran out the back door.

"You can't do that with one arm. I don't know what I was thinking, letting you come out here to haul all this snow," he said. He grabbed the shovel over Lindsay's objections and shoveled the trucks free in no time while Lindsay looked on gratefully. "Remember when I said I didn't have to prove anything to anyone?" he asked when he was finished.

"I remember," she said. It was when she'd asked him if he'd ever seen a Sasquatch.

"Well, neither do you," he said, handing her back the shovel. He went inside to finish his breakfast and Lindsay, considering what he'd said, followed close behind.

When they'd all finished eating, Moose, Hook, and Brian thanked Lindsay for her hospitality and headed on out, letting her know that they'd be back at dinnertime.

Left alone in the house, Lindsay stayed busy. She chased the kitten, did the dishes, made some calls, extracted the kitten from the Christmas tree, swept the kitchen floor, played with the kitten, and cleaned the upstairs bathroom. At lunchtime, she sat down at the kitchen table. Pulling out her phone, she researched New Year's décor. Since Grace had returned, she had been the mastermind behind their fabulous parties, but Lindsay enjoyed digging up ideas as well. She was scrolling along, bookmarking pages as she went, when she suddenly changed course.

Making the barn all pretty wasn't going to mean anything if they didn't have a barn by this time next year.

Grabbing a notebook and pen from the junk drawer, Lindsay took her searches in an entirely new direction. She researched Wisconsin's marital property laws, something she'd been avoiding up until now, afraid of what she might find.

She and Steve would have to split their property 50/50. Everything- the business, the house, and all the land would have to be accounted for. What if he insisted on getting the business? It was where she lived. It was going to be complicated, exactly as she had feared. Grandma had been right; it was realistic to imagine that Lindsay may end up losing everything she held dear, left with some paltry cash.

This was why she'd avoided investigating her options for all those months that Steve was gone. There was a part of her that had always sensed how precarious her position was, and now it had been confirmed. The cold hard truth was staring her in the face. No matter how hard she tried, no matter how much she wished it wasn't true, she could end up being the weak link that allowed her family's heritage to slip away.

Lindsay flipped her notebook shut, stashing it back in the drawer. She had gone into her research expecting to feel nervous but liberated. Instead, she was terrified and more uncertain than ever.

As if sensing her wavering resolve, Steve was back before dinner bearing a gift.

"What's this for?" Lindsay asked.

"I just wanted to give my wife something special."

My wife. Those words sounded foreign coming out of his mouth, as if he was referring to someone else. They didn't have that kind of a relationship anymore, and here he was, trying to force it so quickly.

He handed her the gift. It was wrapped in the same paper as the secret admirer presents. Lindsay's heart sank. So the gifts *had* been coming from Steve. There was no tag this time. She slid open the paper and revealed a wooden recipe box with her maiden name, Antoine, carved into the front.

She surreptitiously nudged the note that had also been tucked into the box deeper into the paper and thanked Steve for his thoughtful gift.

"I knew you would like it. Now you'll have two." He opened his arms for a hug and Lindsay gave him a cursory squeeze. "You probably need an extra with all the recipes you're picking up. I hear you won the bake-off."

"I did. It was a team effort."

"Wow," he chuckled again. "You beat two other competitors. Or was it three this time?"

"Just two," Lindsay said, forcing the corners of her mouth into a smile that didn't reach her eyes.

"Well, you've gotta start somewhere, right?"

"Yes. Gotta start somewhere."

"Do you need anything done tonight? I already put in my time this morning, but I would do something else if you needed me to."

"This gift was all the help I needed. Thank you."

"Any time. I'll come back Thursday." He strolled out.

"We'll see about that," said Lindsay. She took the letter out of the box. It read: *Merry Christmas to the best baker in town. You're an inspiration. Love, Your secret admirer.*

That evening, after their lodgers had settled in for the night, Lindsay and Grace once again met in the living room for a sister meeting.

"So it was you," said Lindsay.

"What was me?" Grace feigned confusion.

"A recipe box? You're the only one who knew that was exactly what I needed."

"Alright, yes, you found me out. It was me completing Operation Christmas Monkey."

"So that's what Christmas Monkey meant...I don't get it."

"I was being sneaky like a monkey."

"Oh yes, that makes sense," she said with a laugh.

Grace had always been drawn to the types of good deeds that could be done without the recipient being the wiser. Lindsay recalled many mornings during their childhood when she woke up early to see that Grace wasn't in bed. She and Grace shared a room, despite the fact that there were plenty of bedrooms in the big old farmhouse for everyone to have their own, with two to spare. The sisters would stay up late spinning tales about invented characters, eyes wide during the scary parts, tears of laughter streaming down their faces when Nobbles or Wimbly or any number of other sprites would make the type of mischief that the girls would never have dared to attempt in real life. In the morning, they could never agree on who had been the first to fall asleep the night before.

Grace was often out of bed early, and Lindsay would go to the window and peek outside, expecting to find her there. Grace would be just visible in the early morning light, flitting from tree to tree in the orchard, filling a basket with crisp red apples or juicy cherries. Other times she'd be farther afield, picking a bouquet of flowers in the meadow. Her little bare legs flew beneath her fluttering pajama gown while her long hair streamed behind her. Lindsay usually went back to sleep. She'd always needed more sleep than her little sister.

When Lindsay woke up later though, Grace would be back in bed, making a show of stretching and rubbing her eyes as if she'd just awoken as well. They'd pad into the kitchen to find a basket of fruit or a vase full of riotous wildflowers on the table and Grace would say, "I wonder where these came from," in her squeaky little voice and make a show of breathing in the heady scent of the bouquet, coming away with a dusting of pollen on her nose or taking a half moon bite out of a burnished apple.

Their parents and Lindsay played along, making guesses as to what sneaky neighbor or autumnal elf had spirited in such precious gifts. It went on for so long that Lindsay was sure that Grace had long since surmised that they knew who was behind the offerings, but no one ever addressed it, and some of the magic lingered long after knowledge of the pretense was shared by all.

"I sneaked it to Arthur, who carved our family name on it, and I picked it up on my lunch break today. Did you find it right away?"

"Steve gave it to me."

"He found it on the porch?"

"Yes, but he *gave* it to me, as in 'Here's a present from your adoring husband.'"

"What?" Grace almost fell out of her chair. "You're kidding."

"I wish."

"Didn't he think the person who gave it to you would mention it at some point?"

"I'm starting to suspect that he considers me to be rather dim-witted." Lindsay puffed up a pillow and hugged it to her chest.

"Good thing you're not. I find that it's not the worst thing in the world to be underestimated."

"He's still lying to me though, even as he says he wants to make amends. I was imagining we'd get to the root of our issues, really hash it out, but by all appearances he just wants to go back to the way things were before."

"And you can't do that. You've changed. I can see how much you've changed every day."

"Thank you, but I still feel guilty, and that's the part that's holding me back now."

"Guilty about what?"

"About giving up on my marriage. What if my hesitance about getting back together drove him to lie to me about the present, and maybe he was sneaking around at Halloween because he was afraid of my reaction when he came back. Besides, he didn't have a great childhood. He didn't have any role models for what a good marriage even looks like."

Grace shook her head, looked Lindsay in the eye and said, "Alright, I have to tell you something. I'm still not sure if I should, but I've regretted holding back for years, and if I don't tell you now I might regret it forever."

Lindsay said nothing, waiting for her sister to reveal whatever had been tormenting her.

Grace hugged her knees. She took a deep breath and began. "Right after you and Steve got engaged, he tried to kiss me."

"What?"

"I'm sorry. I should have told you, but I knew you'd be devastated and I never mustered up the courage. You were so thrilled about planning your wedding."

Lindsay couldn't believe this. "I wouldn't have been if I'd known that. Wait, back up. What exactly happened?"

"It was over the summer, when we were all

here visiting Mom and Dad. I was in my room, and Steve came in and started talking to me, asking me about school. I was sitting on the bed, and he sat down and put his hand on my thigh and tried to kiss me. I pushed him away, of course, and he acted like I'd been the one trying to kiss him. He even threatened to tell you that I was coming onto him if I told you."

"So you didn't tell me, and I went ahead with the wedding like a fool."

"I'm so sorry. I've tried to make it up to you."

Lindsay stared into the cold fireplace. "Can you just go? I need some space."

"Can't we talk about this?"

"Not right now. It's too much."

Grace got up to go. Before she left, she said, "I really am sorry. By the time I worked up the courage to tell you, it was too late. I have to live with that." She walked away, and Lindsay was left alone.

"So do I," Lindsay said in a monotone to no one. Just then she realized she hadn't had the chance to tell Grace that Grandma was gone too. Her wrist was broken, she was going to lose the house, her marriage was officially over, and to top it off, she'd discovered that her own sister had held back information that could've saved her from all this heartache.

Joy jumped onto her lap, curling her body into a horseshoe and stretching out the toes on her little paws so that her claws stuck out like skinny grains of uncooked rice. Lindsay sat in the chair with her kitten while the minute hand on the mantel clock made a full rotation. Too weary to stand, Lindsay's head nodded and she fell asleep.

Chapter Seventeen

In Which a Blue Christmas Becomes a Mysterious One Too

When the clock struck three, Lindsay cracked open her eyes. She should go upstairs to bed. Joy had climbed off her lap and was curled up between two pillows with one paw stretched over her head. Her little pink tongue stuck out between her lips.

Lindsay got up, stretched, and unplugged the tree. Climbing the stairs, she averted her eyes to avoid looking at the accusing stares of her hard-working ancestors.

She crept into her room and shut the door quietly; it slid shut with a soft click. She knew she should go to bed, or she was going struggle the next day, but instead she sat on top of her quilt, staring at her reflection in the window. The armoire loomed behind her.

Getting up, she strode across the room and

threw open its doors. She pulled out the ammo box and marched it into the basement. Wide awake now, Lindsay grabbed a hammer, balanced it on top of the box so she could carry both with one hand, and headed for the barn.

She flipped on the wagon wheel chandelier that hung above the event hall. It illuminated the stage and the beautiful wood walls. The spot where the fire had started was undetectable now, having been fixed thanks to insurance and a talented carpenter.

Lindsay sat down in the middle of the floor and pounded away at the metal hinges of the ammo case, sending flakes of rust flying in every direction. She couldn't steady it, so it slid away from her. She kept pulling it back and whacking it again until one of the hinges cracked open with a snap. One down, one to go.

The other hinge was more stubborn. It flattened and warped, but didn't break. Lindsay groaned in frustration, giving it a mighty whack. It finally broke, and Lindsay stuck her fingers in the base of the lid, scrambling for purchase. The lid, dented and mashed from her attack, wouldn't budge. It was sealed with rust as well.

Lindsay set the box on its side and tapped around the edge more gently, her hands and the floor becoming coated with red-brown dust. During a more aggressive whack, the lid popped open and she tilted the case upright, letting the lid fall back to expose the treasures inside.

A metal chain link bracelet perched atop a dry

leather journal. She picked up the bracelet first. It was engraved with a name: *Charles Wathelet*. This bracelet didn't belong to the hermit; it was her great-grandfather's. Lindsay ran her fingers along his name. There were more engravings on the other side: *We love you*. It must've been from his wife and children.

Her finger brushed a latch on one side and the engraved portion of the chain link bracelet popped open. It was a locket. Two little black and white photos were stacked on top of one another in the bottom half.

A pair of young children smiled up at her. It was Grandma Vivian and her brother Noah. Grandma looked to be about two. Her cheeks were pudgy, her blonde hair curled and pinned away from her face. Noah must've been four when his picture was taken. His haircut, parted neatly to one side, gave him the appearance of a suave little man.

There was a single photo on the other side. Her great-grandmother wore a wool car coat and tilted her head towards a sharply dressed and strikingly handsome man, who looked down at her with adoration. The man was not her great-grandfather.

Lindsay squinted at the little picture. Could she be mistaken? Why would her great-grandpa have a picture of his wife with someone else? No, there was no doubt in Lindsay's mind. Whoever that was, she had never seen that man or his likeness in her entire life.

Chapter Eighteen

In Which Days of Auld Lang Syne are Not as They Once Appeared

L eaving the locket open on her lap, Lindsay gently but urgently lifted out the journal. A branching tree was stamped on the outside. The pages had been held together by a leather string whose ends dangled loosely.

Did the answer to the mystery lie here? Would this notebook provide answers to the questions raised by the bracelet, or leave her even more confused?

Lindsay eased open the journal, careful not to tear its thin yellow pages and read, starting with the first page.

December
1946
At the hospital, they told me I've got nerves, like I don't know. Patton called men like me yellow-bellied, and maybe

he's right. They used to call it something else too, but I figure people have been through enough already, and nerves sounds gentler than shell-shocked. It means the same though, means they think I'm crazy, that there's something wrong with my mind. Thing is, I can tell a guy that I'm here, back home. I'm not over there anymore. I can tell him the fighting's over. It's down to chance that I'm still breathing, that I wasn't the one that stepped on that landmine, or that the shrapnel whizzed past my head and hit the kid behind me. It's not my fault I'm still breathing and all those other guys aren't. I can tell him that. I know it. No, the trouble isn't with my head; it's coming from someplace else. Go back to farming and forget about it, they said, but when I smell the damp soil, that moist earth rips a scab off my heart that barely had a chance to heal. I see a green fly, nothing but a little green fly settling on a cow's tail, and the seam that's formed in my chest is wrenched apart. I'm no good like this. No good to anyone.

July 1947

Told Dorothy to stop coming by. Last time she came around she looked scared, and I could only vaguely remember her previous visit. Told her to stop Vivian from coming out too. Surprised Dot. She must not have known about her visits.

October 1948

Getting cold this week. Leaves turning. Need to figure out better set-up for winter. Dorothy leaves food on stump. Will ask for more blankets. Trying to drink less. Vivian still comes by. Tough to ask her not to. Scared her away. Feel awful, but for her own good.

December 1949

Vivan left gift on stump. Little poured candle. Does she recognize me somehow? Has her mother's heart.

Lindsay wiped tears from her eyes as she read the following years' entries. She followed along as the writing became shakier, sometimes filling page after page of descriptions of the woods or memories of his childhood on the farm. It was the farm that she had grown up on as well. They both knew the ins and outs of the home, the orchard, the barn, and the land intimately.

There was a hillock in the back field where Charles and his brothers would play capture the mountain. There was a loose floorboard in the north-east bedroom, Lindsay's bedroom and his too, where he stashed his loose teeth so the tooth fairy wouldn't abscond with them, flittering away to add them to her faraway castle. There was a clump of cedars just behind the barn, the ones that had somehow been missed by hungry deer, whose branches concealed pirate forts and summer picnics.

He'd taken her great-grandma there the day he'd proposed to her and toddled Grandma Vivian, just Vivian then, through the orchard in the spring, the delicate white petals drifting into her curly blonde mop of hair. He recalled when his son Noah was born. He'd been out on the tractor when his be-loved mother-he could still recall her scent; it was Wright's Pond Lily toilet wash-yelled out to him that it was a boy.

He'd sprinted across the field and up the stairs to behold his beautiful wife holding their little pink son, and he'd sworn to protect them forever. He'd stayed true to that vow until the day he died.

Who was that other man? The one who came home with him from the war and took his name and his place? Why would he have agreed to such a thing? Nothing in the pages of the leather bound journal held the answers to those questions. Had Grandma Vivian ever discovered the truth? If she hadn't, was it Lindsay's place to tell her? She didn't feel she had much choice in the matter. Something like this was too significant to keep quiet.

Lindsay reassembled the box as close to the

way she had found it as possible. She nestled it under her arm and made her way back inside. Upon reaching her room, she lifted the loose floorboard next to the window and stashed the ammunition case inside.

Chapter Nineteen

In Which Jack Frost Blows In

T he following morning, Lindsay woke up and grabbed her phone off the nightstand. She called Steve, not expecting him to pick up. He had never answered a single call from her since he'd left. She was rehearsing the voicemail that she would leave when Steve did pick up, taking her by surprise.

"Hey, I'm coming over tonight. Do you need something?" he asked.

Oh. Well, her basic message was the same in person as it would've been in the voicemail. "Yes, I'd like you to come over, but just to have a discussion with you about a decision I've made about moving forward."

"A decision? I thought we were taking our time with this."

"I did too, but I've gotten more clarity, and I'm not going to be changing my mind."

He was quiet on the other end. "Are you going

to give me some idea of what you're thinking? I don't want to go into this blind."

Like she had been doing for months? "I would like to move forward with getting a divorce."

"What? Where is this coming from all of a sudden? I thought we were going to try to work things out."

Lindsay took a deep breath, trying to steady her nerves and her voice. "Our relationship wasn't right for me. I hope you'll come to understand that it's for the best for both of us."

"Why have I been coming over and helping you out? Were you just trying to get some free labor? I even brought you that snow blower."

The snow blower? That's what he was worried about? This was the part where Lindsay usually felt guilty and apologized. She backed down, and Steve got what he wanted. Today, however, she felt only firmness and resolve. "I wanted to see if we could work things out, but that won't be possible. I'm sorry."

"What changed?"

That was a good question. What had changed? Steve hadn't, and that was the problem. He was still offering her the same circumstances, and she wasn't interested in that anymore. She was going to live, fully and wholeheartedly, as best she could from here on out. If that meant that she would be on her own, that was how it was going to be. It was better than being with someone who didn't respect her. "We want different things," she said.

"Is it someone else? Actually, no. Forget it. Don't answer that. I don't deserve this. You were always in it for yourself. After all I've done for you."

There it was. This was exactly what she was expecting, and precisely why she'd made this decision. "I wish it could've worked out differently, and I wish you well."

"Whatever. That's fine, but I'm coming to get the snow blower right now."

Again with the snow blower? "Alright. Will you bring mine back, please?"

He'd hung up.

Lindsay got out of bed, flung open her curtains, threw on her jeans and sweater, awkwardly pulled her hair into a ponytail (it was nearly impossible with one hand), and ran down the stairs. There were muffins to bake and a smoothie to blend.

Steve pulled up while she prepared breakfast. Should she go out to meet him? Try to soften the blow one last time? No. He wasn't interested in hearing what she had to say. She'd only get hurt if she put herself in his way right now.

He roughly lugged the ancient orange snow blower out of the back of his truck and yanked it into the garage. On the other hand, maybe she should head out to make sure it was all in one piece. She slipped on her boots and ran outside, immediately wishing she'd put on her jacket. It was so cold the inside of her nose froze immediately after she'd taken her first breath.

She jogged into the garage, where Steve was rummaging around beneath the tarp that covered their camping gear. What was he doing? Lindsay cleared her throat and Steve straightened up and turned around. "Just looking for my tent," he muttered. "I'll leave it for now."

He marched past her. She needed to move out of the way to avoid a smack from his shoulder. He wheeled his shiny new snow blower into his truck and drove away without saying another word. It was only the first step of many, but it was a step forward, and that's what was important. Lindsay went back inside, plugged in the kitchen tree, flipped on the radio, and sang along.

Grace was up and in the kitchen before the lodgers that morning. She must not have had to work that day. She'd already showered and was dressed in a gray henley topped with a cute pink cardigan.

She helped Lindsay get breakfast started with only a sheepish, "Hey."

Lindsay put her hand on Grace's shoulder. "I want to talk to you about last night, if that's okay."

"Yeah. I'm sorry. I feel terrible, but I didn't know what to do."

Lindsay didn't know if Grace was referring to now or back then, but either way she could relate. "I know. I understand. I thought about it a lot, and I'm not sure if it would've made any difference if you'd have told me what happened before the wedding. I shouldn't have married Steve, for a whole bunch of reasons, but I did. You don't need to feel guilty about anything. I'm the one who needs to figure out what to do."

AMANDA SCHWANTES

"Thank you. But you can get help from me, you know."

The sisters hugged, and Lindsay said, "I know I can, and that means the world to me."

"Seriously, be honest about how you're doing. We're a team now."

"We've been a team, and that's part of what I wanted to talk to you about too. I told Steve I want a divorce."

"You did? Congratulations. I know that sounds weird, but..."

"No. It doesn't. Thank you. I feel really good about it. I don't know if we can save the farm and the inn, though. Steve owns half of it, and I haven't had time to figure out how this will all end up. If we can save it, do you want to go in on it with me? Be official partners?"

Grace jumped up and down and clapped her hands, "Yes! I would love that."

"You don't have to decide right away."

"But I've already decided. This is fantastic. We could even specialize, like Chloe and Betsy. I love planning the events, and you're an amazing baker and chef and hostess."

It did sound ideal, but Lindsay hoped she hadn't spoken too soon. If they ended up losing the farm, and that looked like a good possibility, especially if Steve made things difficult, Grace would be all the more disappointed if she had her hopes up.

"I'm going to try my absolute best to keep our house in the family," Lindsay promised. "If only I had

200

proof that Steve started the fire..."

Grace nodded. "It certainly would help your case, and all the evidence points to him, but I think we need to let it go. Dave can't share everything with me, but he said that Steve was their prime suspect. They needed more to go on though, and there just wasn't enough evidence."

Lindsay knew that what her sister was saying was true, but maybe the police had missed something. "I wish that camera in the orchard worked at night. The trail from where he was parked to the barn would've run him right past it."

"Sorry if this is a silly question, but did you check the camera to make sure?" Grace set the muffins on the table and poured the smoothies into tall glasses.

"I did. That's part of why I think he might've passed by. The camera took a single picture around the time he would've been there, but the flash didn't work. The photo is completely black."

Grace sat down in the chair and propped her elbows on the table, resting her head in her hands as she thought. "What if the fire really was a fluke?" Lindsay started to object and Grace held up her hands. "Hear me out for a second. I'm not saying the chances are good, but an electrical fire could start any time, right? Steve admits to having been there, so even if you had photographic evidence in your hand that he was in the orchard that night, it wouldn't change anything."

Lindsay joined Grace at the table, picking up a pumpkin muffin and taking a bite. It was delicious.

The guys were going to love them. It was probably smart to get them while the getting was good.

"Wait...what about his phone?" said Lindsay.

"What about it?"

"How did he know how to start an electrical fire? He did the electrical work on the barn, so it wouldn't have been a complete mystery, but I would bet almost anything he needed to do some research in advance."

Grace brightened up. "You're right. He'd probably need to know something about how fires are investigated, too. Even though his plan didn't work, he was able to cover his tracks."

This was promising, but there were quite a few glaring problems. The most obvious was how they would gain access to his phone. And once they did, how would they search his browsing history? Maybe Grace knew. Lindsay asked her and Grace wrinkled her forehead, thinking. She looked like their mom when she did that, but Lindsay wasn't about to inform her of that fact.

"I can figure out how to search his phone," said Grace, "but is this the best way to go? I'm not sure it's legal, so even if we do find something, it might not help. It may end up creating more problems for us instead of the other way around."

Lindsay saw her point. "Let's just consider it for now. I need to do some more research. Maybe something like that won't be necessary. If it looks bad enough though, I may come back to the idea."

"Fair enough," said Grace. "Let's keep it in

mind. What are you up to today?"

"I'm going to dig up the owner's manual for the old snow blower and fix it for good this time. My goal is that, by the time I'm finished with it, it'll be better than new. I really think I can do it. I'm inviting Grandma back too. I hope she'll agree."

Grace had just taken a bite of muffin, and she coughed in surprise. When she'd recovered she asked, "Back? Did she leave? Why didn't I notice that?"

Lindsay explained what had happened between her and Grandma, but left out the part about the shocking discovery she'd made last night. If Grandma knew the identity of her father, she hadn't told either of them. She may not have wanted them to know.

Grace looked sad. "Grandma has a big heart. All of this has been more difficult for her than she lets on."

"I agree, but at the same time I don't regret standing up to her. I needed my decision about Steve to be my own. I needed to stand up to him too, for that matter."

"Yeah," Grace said. "I can see that. You're becoming quite brave, facing off with Grandma and Steve in the span of twenty-four hours."

Lindsay smiled. She felt quite brave. "What about you? What are you up to today? You look really nice."

"Why thank you. Dave and I planned to go up north to the Christmas market in Fish Creek, but now that I know that Grandma might not be here, maybe I should cancel."

"I appreciate that, but I'm getting pretty good at doing things around here with one hand. Would you be able to chop the veggies for dinner again, though? I should be all set then."

"Yes I will. Happy to help, partner."

Lindsay was optimistic that team sister would prevail.

Chapter Twenty

In Which Grandma Sheds More Light on the Murky Past

Lindsay pulled the box out from beneath the floorboards. Her grease stained fingers trembled. She'd tried to wash it off after working on the snow blower, but it wouldn't budge. She'd have to get used to it. The blower still needed a lot of work, and most of it couldn't be done with one hand, but it was going to run like a dream if it took her all winter to get it there.

The box, sitting on the rug in front of the armoire now, looked more battered than ever before, even as its significance had increased exponentially in Lindsay's mind. Were the secrets it held a surprise only to her, or would her grandma be staggered by them as well? Speaking of Grandma, she should've been here twenty minutes ago. Maybe she'd changed her mind about coming after all.

Lindsay had called Grandma that morning, telling her everything that had happened between her and Steve. Grandma didn't express any kind of surprise, just said, "A leopard can't change its spots, no matter how much you might want it to." And in this case, Lindsay had to agree.

What Lindsay didn't tell her, however, was what she'd discovered inside an old ammo box buried in Hiram's shack.

The back door squeaked open and Grandma called out, "I'm back and better than ever."

Lindsay joined her in the kitchen. Grandma wore another festive outfit, a sweater this time, adorned with bells and tinsel. A thick green beaded necklace draped to her belly button and matching earrings dangled beneath her fresh haircut. Lindsay didn't want to tell her. It wasn't too late to put the box back under the floor and leave it there for the next generation to find, if there was a next generation.

But no, Grandma deserved to know the truth, if she didn't already.

"I'll be right back, Grandma," she said, turning back to the landing, picking up the case, and setting it on the table. She'd expose the truth right away, afraid that she'd lose her courage if she didn't. "It's great to see you," Lindsay said, giving Grandma a hug.

Grandma hugged her back. "I'm sorry. I got a little carried away with my own self-righteous indignation. You've got a good head on your shoulders. I should've trusted you to figure out what you needed to do on your own. Besides, believe it or not, you come from a long line of women who don't like to be told what to do."

Lindsay wholeheartedly believed that. "Thank you. It's taken me a long time to trust myself."

Grandma pulled off her coat then spotted the box on the table. "What do you have there? It looks like my dad's, but this one's much worse for the wear." She moved to open the case, but Lindsay stopped her.

"Wait. Before you do that, I have to tell you something."

Grandma turned to face her, smiling. She had no idea what was coming. When she saw the look on Lindsay's face though, Grandma turned serious.

"I found this box buried in Hiram's shack the day we went out there with Brian," said Lindsay. "There's a bracelet inside, and a journal, and...the things those items suggest are surprising."

"What do you mean?"

Lindsay had planned to tell her everything first, but that didn't feel right somehow. She trusted her instincts and let Grandma open the box. She pulled out the bracelet.

Grandma read the inscription on one side. "Charles?" She squinted and took her reading glasses out of her purse, putting them on. "This was my father's? I don't understand." She ran the metal chains over her soft wrinkled palm then flipped it over, just as Lindsay had done.

"It's a locket," Lindsay explained. She gently popped it open and her Grandma smiled at the pictures of her and Noah.

"He was always such a beautiful boy. Look at

those eyes. I was pretty cute too, if I do say so myself. This is wonderful. I'm pleased as punch to have it. I wonder why it was buried all the way out there..."

Next, she took in the larger photo on the opposite side. She didn't register what she was seeing right away. "My mother loved that wool car coat. She was a hard working farm woman, but she sure did love to dress up, and my father..."

She looked up in confusion. "That's Hiram."

"I thought it must be."

"But how could you have known that? What was he doing with my mother?" She closed the clasp and read the name on the locket once more, confirming what she'd seen. "The bracelet has my father's name on it."

Lindsay picked up the journal and handed it to her. Was she doing the right thing? She still wasn't sure. She wanted to run into the woods and rebury the box and the secrets it held, to shield her Grandmother from learning the truth. At the same time, Lindsay was certain that she, herself, would want to know the identity of her own father if their roles were reversed.

Grandma sat down and opened the journal. She started to read the initial entry then looked up at Lindsay and shook her head. "That poor man. The attitudes that people had back then...well, some still do. He needed help, and he never got it. He felt ashamed." She shook her head. "I'm still not understanding though."

Lindsay flipped the page and prompted her to

read on. As she read, she covered her mouth with her hand. "Oh my goodness. After all this time. It was him all along."

She hadn't known.

Lindsay walked closer, resting her hands on her grandma's trembling shoulders. She sat down beside her and waited as her grandma read page after page of her father's memories.

When she had finished reading she said. "I never had a clue. Never an inkling. My father-the man I thought of as my father-wasn't a warm man. He and my mother didn't share much affection, but he seemed to be doing what he could." She looked into space, as if trying to recall the signs she must've missed.

After a long silence she said, "As I've told you, my father never spoke of the war. We didn't understand why he had those nightmares, why he'd get so quiet and strange sometimes. After he died, I sent away for his service records. I guess I wanted to understand him better. What I got were the records for Charles Wathelet, who I now know is the man I called Hiram, the hermit in the woods. It turns out he was an Army forward observer. It was a very dangerous job. He sneaked up to enemy lines, as close as he could get, so he could radio in their precise location.

"One night, somewhere in Germany-the specific location had been blacked out-he and his company of 120 men ran into an SS division after crossing a river. They were trapped. Half the men were taken down by machine gun fire and mortar shells before they knew what hit them. My father stood tall and encouraged them to push on. They overran those Nazis, and routed them from a nearby village too. By then, only a quarter of the men were left." She looked down and shook her head. "All those young men, gone just like that.

"At the edge of the village, an SS mortar round exploded near Charles and another member of his company. Shrapnel sliced through the other man's throat, and my father carried him all the way to the closest aid station, two and a half miles away. He saved that man's life before running right back out there to help secure the village.

"He was a hero." Her voice cracked. "It all makes sense now. The man I always thought of as my father had a jagged scar running from the center of his Adam's apple to the back of his neck. He never talked about how he got it, and I never dared ask."

Lindsay sat there with her grandma for a long time, neither woman saying a word. What was there to say? The man who left for the war as her father returned to his home as a recluse, leaving his family to be headed by another man, likely the man he saved on that long ago day on the other side of the world.

Finally, Lindsay spoke. "How could something like that have been kept a secret? People here would've known Charles all his life."

Her grandma maintained her puzzled, faraway gaze as she said, "I'm certain they realized what had happened, whether it was explained directly or not. But people didn't ask so many questions back then.

They surely had their own heartaches to mend, their own farms to maintain. If the arrangement was working, perhaps they didn't think it was their place to notice. There's no one left to ask now, so we'll likely never know."

"Do you think your brother knew?"

Grandma shook her head, her hands caressing the shape of the branching tree on the soft leather journal. "No. I'm certain he didn't. He never went out to visit with Hiram like I did. Noah joined the man I considered to be my father in pretending that he wasn't there. He wasn't mean spirited about it, just identified with our father and followed his lead... I wonder what his name really was, and if he had any family. Did he have parents wondering about him somewhere? It's all so..."

She trailed away and closed her eyes. When she opened them, her gaze was clearer, as if she had come back to the present "My mother though, she kept an eye on Hiram. I wish I could talk to her now. I can't imagine what she thought about all this. My father, the real Charles, must have thought she needed a man on the farm after the boys came home, but from the way she talked, she and the recruits from the Women's Land Army had this place running like clockwork throughout the war."

The Women's Land Army? Was that a real thing, or just Grandma's name for the women who came to help on the farm while the men were away? "You've never mentioned how your mom managed the farm on her own. I'm surprised I never thought to ask."

The ghost of a smile drifted across Grandma's eyes and settled on her lips. "Oh, yes. With the men off fighting, there was going to be a food shortage, worse than there was already. So, the government set up a program to get women into the fields. Those bureaucrats got there kicking and screaming, and some of the old timers didn't like it, but they didn't have much of a choice if we wanted to eat. The women-secretaries, housewives, teachers-took a short course at the college and then got bussed up here to the country to work on the farms.

"Some of them had never left the city, but my mother had them driving the tractor and milking cows on day one. You should've heard the stories she'd tell about some of them." She wiped a tear from her eye, and whether it was one of amusement or sadness, Lindsay couldn't tell. "I don't remember it well, but she set up a daycare in the house for the ones that had kids. Old Mrs. Jacquemart would come over and watch us little ones while the women worked from dawn to dusk. Most of the stories are in my mother's letters to Charles. I'll have to share them with you some time."

"I would love that."

"I can't believe I somehow neglected to pass along those tales. I know better than anyone how much can be lost if you leave them until it's too late." She opened the journal again, scanning the entries randomly, as if searching for clues. "I may never know the true name of the man who became my father after the war, but he showed me what love is, duty too. He didn't have to come here and do what he did. They were both good men doing the best they could, looking out for us as well as they were able. I've been around long enough to know that you don't take that kind of love for granted. Not ever."

She clutched the journal to her chest. "My suitcase is in the car. I'll get it later, if you'll have me."

"Of course I will. Stay as long as you want."

Grandma wagged a finger at her. "Careful what you wish for. You might not be able to get rid of me if I get used to hanging around here too long. For now, I'm going to head upstairs with this little book and spend some more time with my father. Well, one of my fathers anyway." She smiled and padded out of the room in her stocking feet.

Lindsay sat alone at the table with the box. The chain link bracelet made an s-curve across the top of the wooden table. A square of sunlight, streaming through the widow, fell on the photos in the locket. Lindsay considered the handsome couple and their smiling children once more. Her great-grandparents made heart-wrenching decisions to do what they thought was right with what they had available. How could Lindsay honor them now?

She picked up the bracelet and lay it across her wrist. It was too small to go around the cast, but when she tried to fasten it on her left wrist, the fingers of her right hand weren't nimble enough to clasp it. Instead, she slid it into her pocket for safekeeping.

Pushing her chair away from the table, Lindsay

slid on her boots and opened the front door. A fluffy white pine wreath, carefully woven together with branches from her own towering trees, hung there as a greeting to visitors. She stepped outside, lifted it off its hook, strung it through her arm, and quickly closed the door before Joy could sneak her way out.

The front steps were clear of snow, but Lindsay still walked down them cautiously, not trusting her balance like she used to. She crunched down the driveway, passed the barn with its identical wreath in a much larger scale, and stepped over a drift of snow into the orchard. The midwinter sun stretched the shadows of the trees along her path, creating streaks of light and dark over the snow.

Little drifts and hillocks in the field beyond the orchard cowered like snow covered gnomes, slumbering away in winter dormancy. She passed them all, tapping one on its oversized cap. When she reached the forest the going became easier. Much of the snow had been trapped in the boughs of the trees above her.

Lindsay breathed in the sharp sun warmed scent of ice draped pines. It was easy to avoid the larger clumps of brambles that popped up here and there in the undergrowth, but every now and then a long stalk would sneak up on her, catching on her jacket and making the scraping sound of tearing nylon. It didn't matter. The jacket was old, and Lindsay had something important to do.

She reached the old shack and ducked inside. It looked even smaller now that she understood a fraction of all it had contained. "I'm sorry, Great-

Grandpa," she said. She wished him peace, wished that his memory would be a gift to those who had known him and all who were touched by his legacy. Most would never know who he was or what he had done, but they would go on because of him nevertheless.

Lindsay backed out of the shack and closed the door. She hung the wreath there, on a sliver of wood that would serve as a hook. She stepped back and took it in for a moment before turning around and hiking back through the forest towards home.

Chapter Twenty-One

In Which Faithful Friends Gather Together

The last meeting of the year for the Demeter Society was held at Chloe's house at the edge of town. Grace and Betsy had been invited to attend, but had no idea that they were going to be asked to join as well.

When they arrived, Chloe's dog Marshmallow jumped on Lindsay, giving her cheek a hearty lick.

"I'm so sorry," said Chloe. "We're still working on that."

Lindsay didn't mind. Besides, she probably smelled like kitten. Grace and Lindsay had been the last to arrive. They sat down on kitchen chairs that Chloe had pulled into her living room for the big event.

Chloe's tree was set up in one corner of the room. A wooden nativity was spread across the mantle, gorgeous in its simplicity. Lindsay wondered if Arthur had carved it as well.

Now that everyone was there, Chloe stood and clapped her hands. "I have an important announcement to make. For the first time ever, we would like to induct two new members to the Demeter Society in a single evening. Betsy and Grace, would you come forward if you accept your nomination for membership?"

Both women looked startled but pleased. Betsy ran up first and Chloe made an imaginary microphone with her fist, which her sister gladly accepted. "I would be thrilled to join this eminent collaboration of women and would like to make a speech," said Betsy.

Chloe sat down to listen, and Betsy carried on without her microphone. "I'm so proud of Chloe and thrilled that Bare Roots Tools will be expanding across the country. She was also wise enough to put me in charge of customer relations, which I love and she can't stand, so win-win. The Demeter Society is amazing and I can't wait to be involved in your projects as well. Thank you." She curtseyed and sat down.

Everyone clapped as Grace came to the fore. "This is so unexpected," she said. "I would be honored to join you. A year ago if you'd told me I'd be moving back to the family homestead I wouldn't have believed it, but now that I'm here, I wouldn't have it any other way. Thank you for making me so welcome. You are all amazing women." Her speech was met with more applause.

Grace sat down, and Lindsay gave her an encouraging smile.

"Welcome to the group guys," said Chloe. "We had a really exciting year, and I thought it would be fun for each of us to discuss our successes, and also things we envision happening next year, either for ourselves or the group. If you have any requests or ideas, you can share them and we can build a discussion from there. What do you think?"

They nodded their approval. "Great. Who wants to go first?" she asked. When no one volunteered she shrugged and said, "Okay, you twisted my arm." Chloe sat back down and excitedly shared her news. "My partnership with Superior Engineering has been a huge success. They're marketing geniuses, and we're developing some really exciting new products. They're still in the works, so I'm not supposed to say too much, but I'm hoping that you guys will be willing to be my guinea pigs."

"I will for sure," said Lindsay. Chloe's pruning shears had saved her wrist this summer. She never realized how large and unwieldy her old set was until she held one that was designed for smaller hands.

"You're going to be really excited about a few of our ideas...but don't ask me what they are. It's going to be a surprise." Chloe waited while everyone quietly honored her request. "Fine. I'll tell you. But only because I know you're not going to stop badgering me if I don't. So, there I was, partnering with a quirky yet compellingly brilliant industrial engineer..."

"Chloe," Bea said, "you know how much I usually love your stories, but I have to get up shockingly early to milk the goats. Will you just tell us what you're working on?"

Chloe looked reluctant, but Bea had a point. They were all busy women. "Fine, we're designing a walk-behind tiller. It's really high tech and amazing and you're going to love it. We're also working on a wheel barrow and a farm cart with the help of a grant I received from the USDA."

"Sign me up," said Lindsay, raising her hand. She loved it already. The straw bales she often used for seating at her events were unwieldy and dense, and she couldn't afford to throw out her back on top of everything else. A farm cart would be a game changer.

"You got it," said Chloe. The pride she had in her work shone in her eyes. "I guess that covers what I did, and what I'm going to do. Anybody else?"

Lindsay had an idea she wanted to share. It had come to her only yesterday. Would everyone else think it was as brilliant as she had? The only way she could find out was to share it. Even if no one else was interested, Lindsay would move forward with the plan herself.

"I'll go," she said. "First, I want to say thank you to all of you. This has been a challenging year for me, but you guys have been there with encouragement, food, and all kinds of help. I've tried to put on a brave face, but it's often been even more difficult than I've let on, and I couldn't have done it without your support." She looked at each one of them in turn.

"We're so happy to help," said Bea.

"You guys are awesome," said Lindsay. "Also,

I'm going forward with my divorce. I feel confident that it's the right thing to do, but the future of my house is in question."

Bea and Sarah gasped. Both of their family farms were nearly as old and long-held as Lindsay's. They understood the significance of what she was saying.

She didn't want them to feel sorry for her, but she could be facing some difficulties in the coming year, and she was working on standing up and being honest. "On the positive side though, Grace and I are going to be partners, and we'll do all we can to keep everything together."

All of the women clapped for them, and Lindsay was overwhelmed with emotion. No matter what happened with the farm, she was going to be alright. She had her friends, her family, and her wits. Chloe whooped. "You two are going to go so far, you'll be standing here this time next year saying that today was the start of something wonderful. I know it."

Lindsay smiled. "I so hope you're right. I have another idea too. It came to me just the other day, so I haven't had a lot of time to look into the details, but I wondered if any of you had considered hiring military veterans to help out with our businesses."

They all looked to each other. Apparently no one else had ever thought about it. They turned back to Lindsay with interested expressions, and she explained what she'd worked out so far.

"I've done a very little bit of research, and rural veterans are often interested in getting involved in farming. They have a relatively high unemployment rate, especially female vets in our area, and we have a need for help. It takes a special kind of person to do well in the military. It's a tough job and so is farming, as we all know. These people have determination and we have knowledge…it seems like it could be really beneficial all around. I'll keep you posted when I learn more about how it works. It sounds like there's a program through the VA. The veterans would receive a stipend to work for us, in addition to what we could pay."

She looked around the room, gauging her friends' reactions. It had seemed like such a wonderful idea, but it was hard to say what they would think.

"I love it," said Sarah, without hesitation. "We have so much to offer here, and we could all use the help. It's an absolutely lovely idea." Everyone else nodded along as she spoke. It was unanimous. Lindsay would carry on with looking into the possibilities. How exciting.

She told them a little about the Women's Land Army as well and her great-grandma's letters. Grandma Vivian would attend the next meeting and share some of their stories, if everyone was interested. That idea was met with nearly equal enthusiasm.

Lindsay and Grandma had shared Charles's story with Grace the night before. They all agreed that his identity wouldn't go beyond their family circle. They weren't ashamed of what had happened, but they weren't sure how much of the story any of those involved would have wanted to be shared.

Did Charles have any inkling that his journal and bracelet would ever be found by those who lived on the property after him? Perhaps, but none of them would ever know for sure. Lindsay liked to think that he had faith that his family would be there for many more generations, that someone like her would find his journal and recover the truth of who he really was and what he had done with his one precious life.

Betsy volunteered next. She sat up ramrod straight. "I have something to say. I've been informed by Chloe that everyone already knows, but I haven't said it out loud to most of you yet. Here it goes: I'm going to be a mom next year." She smiled at them all uncertainly. When her gaze reached Sarah, her face fell. Sarah wasn't looking at her. She was digging in her bag instead. Had she missed what Betsy had said, or was she ignoring the news?

Sarah pulled a soft looking package out of her purse. It was wrapped in tissue paper and tied with a ribbon. She carried it over to Betsy and set it in her lap. "This is for you," said Sarah.

"Oh, thank you," said Betsy.

"You can open it," Sarah replied.

Betsy laughed. "Of course I'll open it. Sorry, I haven't told many people yet. It's still kind of surreal." She untied the ribbon and the paper fell away. Inside was a light yellow crocheted blanket, as fuzzy as a baby chick. She stood up, set the blanket on the chair, and Betsy and Sarah hugged in the middle of their circle of friends.

"Thank you. Thank you so much," Betsy whispered into Sarah's hair.

On the way home that night, Lindsay filled Grace in on the new information she'd discovered about what may happen to their home in the divorce. "If Steve agrees to it, I can give him half the value of what we actually own."

"But how would you do that? The house and the farm are worth much more than what you paid for them. I can't even imagine how much money you'd have to come up with."

"That's what I'd thought at first too, but most of it's owned by the bank, really. I'd only owe him half of our actual assets, and no offense, but that's really not all that much."

"That's great. It sounds like there should be no problem then."

Lindsay wasn't so sure. "I doubt it's going to be that easy. He put a lot of work into all of this. I have the feeling he won't be happy about how much he'd end up walking away with."

Grace stared out her window, thinking. "What can you do though?"

Lindsay was afraid to vocalize what she'd been considering. Once she said it out loud, she might actually go through with it. Was it such a terrible idea though? Justice hadn't been served as far as she was concerned. "I have a plan..."

"Yes?"

"I want to check his phone. Even if we find something that we can't legally use, I'll know he started the fire, and he'll know I know."

Grace sighed and shook her head. "I don't think that's a good idea."

"I know. It probably isn't, but how long am I going to have to be looking over my shoulder, afraid of what he might do next? I don't trust him. Even if all it does is gets him to leave me in peace, it will have been worth it."

Grace was quiet. A car passed them going the other way with its brights on. Lindsay squinted and tilted her head towards her sister. Suddenly, Grace grabbed Lindsay's arm. "Pull over," she said. "I need to tell you something."

"What? What do you mean?" Lindsay veered over to the side of the road and parked. She looked at her sister, who had clasped her hands together, holding them in front of her mouth. She was trembling. "What is it? What happened?" Grace wouldn't look at her. "If you know something, I need you to tell me."

Grace slapped her hands into her lap and turned to face Lindsay. "You won't find anything on Steve's phone. He didn't start the fire. I did."

Chapter Twenty-Two

In Which a Grinch was Nearly Outsmarted by Gracie Lou Who

L indsay punched off the radio. "What do you mean, you did? You started the fire? The one that would have burned down our beautiful barn? Why?" There had to be a reason, some strange reason that Grace was saying this now, because it couldn't possibly be the truth.

"I wanted Steve out of our life. He was ruining everything, terrorizing you," Grace whispered. She looked out the window again, offering Lindsay a view of the back of her head. Lindsay had to strain to hear her. "I thought if I framed him, he'd go to jail and pay for the damages, and we'd get the insurance money. All our problems would be solved." She didn't say more.

Lindsay didn't understand. Something didn't add up. "Why are you saying this? You couldn't have done it. It's not possible."

Grace turned to face her. She looked pale and drawn in the green glow of the dashboard lights. "I did though. I'm the one who learned how to start an electrical fire and cover my tracks. I erased the history from my own phone, but I assure you it was there."

"But why would Steve have been at the house that night? He would've told the police if you'd gotten him there somehow."

"You don't have to believe me, but I did it."

Lindsay didn't want this to be true. All this time, her sister had been lying to her, letting her think it had been Steve. "How could you? That barn is irreplaceable. You could've been the one who ended up arrested. More importantly, you could've killed someone. Chloe and Arthur ended up in there to put it out."

"I know that. I wasn't thinking straight." Grace raised her voice now. "What were you going to do though? Wait around for Steve to give you a call and let you know when he was going to stop stalking us? When he was going to give you permission to move on with your life? One of us needed to take action, and it didn't look like it was going to be you, so I took matters into my own hands."

"That's not fair, and it didn't give you the right to do what you did. Nothing does."

"I know that now. I regretted it the moment I saw you and Chloe that night. It could've been so much worse. As it is, I'm going to need to work on forgiving myself. I still might be able to use this to make things right."

Lindsay doubted that. This couldn't be any help to them at all; if nothing else, she needed to start praying that Steve never discovered the truth. "Does anyone else know it was you?" Grace was dating a police officer now. He didn't know, did he? Could he have been in on it?

"No. No one knows but you and me."

"I still don't understand. It doesn't add up. What was Steve doing there?"

Grace fiddled with her seat belt. She looked out the window again and then back at Lindsay. "You know that painting of Great-Grandma's, the one of the three women?"

Yes. Lindsay adored that painting. It was hanging over the couch, covered in garland as they spoke. She nodded.

"Well, you know how you told me that it was painted by a student of Vladimir Rousseff?"

"Yes...she was a friend of the family." Where was Grace going with this?

"It turns out, after Rousseff left Door County, he became a well known muralist. Many of his murals were eventually painted over, his paintings sold to private collectors. Until recently, most of them had been lost, until a small group who had an interest in his work started researching their whereabouts. One of his smaller paintings was uncovered in a private home in Fish Creek. It sold for over seven hundred thousand dollars."

Wow. That was a lot of money, but what did this have to do with her little painting, or with Steve?

Grace continued. "I called Steve the day before the fire and told him I was an antique dealer who had stayed at the bed and breakfast."

"You called him from your phone?"

"No. I used someone else's and blocked the number. I'd prefer not to say whose; they didn't know what I was doing."

Fair enough. "And he believed you?"

"Apparently. I said you had a rare painting, and you had no idea of its worth."

"You were an antique dealer who had figured out how to contact him somehow and was calling from a blocked number?" Was Steve really this dense or was Grace that skilled an actor? Either way, it was shocking.

"I told him I needed to stay undercover. I'd heard about your separation, and had a buyer who was willing to pay nearly a million dollars for the painting. I offered to split the money with him if he'd help me 'acquire' it."

"That still doesn't explain what he was doing in the orchard," said Lindsay.

"I'm getting to that. I said that I'd meet him in the middle of the orchard that night. He'd let himself in, get the painting, and then hand it over to me. From there, I would deliver it to a ready buyer while he left the state for a month or two with the hope he'd be out of the way, and therefore above suspicion, when you'd noticed the painting was gone."

Lindsay couldn't believe this plan had even almost worked. It sounded like something out of a movie, or a Scandinavian thriller perhaps. Steve did like to imagine that he was some kind of tragic hero. How had Grace known? But something still didn't add up... "No one would have known he was there, not if Chloe and Arthur hadn't shown up."

"They would have, if the trail camera had been working properly. I'd only tested it during the day, when it was working fine. After all that planning, a silly oversight like that wrecked everything. Steve even walked right past it. I was watching him from behind some bushes. I heard it click, but the flash didn't go off, and that's when I knew my plan was doomed.

"It had already been set into motion though. I couldn't turn back, especially not when I heard Arthur and Chloe coming up the drive. Steve heard them too. He ran back to his truck while Arthur and Chloe checked the back door then dashed into the barn and put out the fire. I sneaked back inside and threw on my pajamas before anyone could even suspect I'd been out. You know what happened from there."

Lindsay rubbed her temples, covering her face with her hand. There had been countless times this year when she found herself in a moment that was so unexpected, so outlandish, that she froze up, unable to see a way forward. There was no pattern to follow, no precedent. Needless to say, this was one of those times.

"You said you could make things right. What did you mean?" Lindsay asked her sister, who had gone back to staring out the window.

"I texted Steve later, while he was in Idaho and told him that the buyer backed out and I'd changed my mind about trying a second time. I said I thought it was too risky because of the amount of money involved. He never responded. I was afraid that he was onto me, but when he came back suddenly, full of remorse, I drew another conclusion: he was going to work his way back into the house and try to steal the painting himself."

The sisters looked at each other in the dark. How had this all been going on right under Lindsay's nose without her being aware of any of it? She had never thought of herself as naïve or gullible, but in the past year she'd been completely blindsided by an affair, abandonment, an arson plot, and an attempted art heist. What next? Was Grandma some kind of mafia kingpin? Only time would tell.

"I still don't see how any of this helps us. Unless he took it tonight, the painting is still there, and Steve hasn't done anything wrong, not legally anyway."

"But he still thinks the painting is valuable," Grace explained. "He's sure to ask for it in the divorce. He'll probably say it has sentimental value or something. You can reluctantly agree to part with it. He'll be over the moon, walking away with half your assets and a rare painting. You can finally move on with your life. It's more than he deserves."

"I actually do love that painting though."

"So do I, but it's the price we'll have to pay."

"You know I can't go into business with you

now, right?" Lindsay hated to break it to her-she was devastated about it herself-but this wasn't the kind of thing one just got over in a day or two.

Grace looked aghast. "What do you mean?"

"What do you mean, what do I mean? You showed terrible judgment. I love you; you're my sister, but what you did was so far out of line."

"I know that. Of course I do. I've never even considered doing anything like that before, and I never will again. I wasn't thinking straight. It was crazy around here. I just wanted it to be over."

"I can relate. I felt the same way, but it scares me that you were even capable of this."

Grace looked as though she understood, but it was a huge disappointment. "I'm sorry. Would you like me to leave?"

"Do you want to?"

"No, but it's going to be difficult to stick around if you're distrustful and suspicious of me. Not that I blame you, but I think you understand what I mean."

"I do. I'd like you to decide if staying is the right thing. I want to trust you again, but I need some time, maybe a lot of it. Going into business together is a huge leap of faith."

"I'll think about it."

They sat together in the quiet car, the warmth of the heater insulating them from the dark and cold outside. There was nothing more to say, so neither of them said anything more as Lindsay pulled onto the road and drove them home.

Chapter Twenty-Three

In Which Weenies are Roasting on an Open Fire

It was Christmas Eve. Lindsay sat down with a book and a cat on her lap, side by side. The fire crackled, the stockings were hung, and snow drifted from the sky outside the window. In accordance with long-held tradition, Grandma was making lunch today. The smell of freshly baked bread wafted out of the kitchen and into the living room along with the strains of an orchestral holiday tune.

This evening it would be Grace and Lindsay's turn to get cooking. In the tumult of the past week, Lindsay hadn't been quite as prepared for their Christmas Eve dinner as she would've liked, but she'd gone out this morning to get the remaining ingredients and the turkey was already baking in the oven. It was time to put up her feet and...

"Hey there." It was Moose. "You got any weenie roasters?"

"Excuse me?" Lindsay asked, taken by surprise

at the question and the sudden appearance of Moose in the middle of the day. The guys were usually out all afternoon, although they were planning to be around tomorrow for the Christmas festivities.

"You know, a weenie roaster, like a long pointy metal stick we could use to cook hot dogs over the fire. We had some, but I can't find them."

Oh. A weenie roaster. Right. "I think we have some in the garage. I'll take a look." Lindsay stood and Joy reluctantly leaped off her lap and bounced towards the tree, taking a swipe at a low hanging bulb. "Are you having a fire?"

"Yup. We do it every year. We've got to have hot dogs and marshmallows and a kale salad with microgreens and green goddess vinaigrette. I hope you don't mind if we borrow your blender to make the dressing. It's Brian's specialty."

Lindsay led him through the kitchen, passing Grandma on the way. "I don't mind at all, it's her you're going to have to worry about." Grandma Vivian was dashing around the kitchen stirring sauces on the stove and checking something in the oven.

"What about me?" Grandma asked. She turned around with a dripping spoon in one hand and an oven mitt on the other.

"Well," said Moose, "we're wondering if we can borrow a section of your kitchen right quick. We're making a salad for our Christmas Eve lunch."

"And not eat with us? I wouldn't hear of it."

"It's just..." Moose shifted uneasily where he stood. Apparently the guys had already encountered the dangers involved in standing up to Grandma. He told her about their camp fire tradition.

She threw her hands in the air and a spot of gravy flew across the room and smacked the window. "I love it. We're in."

They were? Lindsay had been looking forward to gourmet feast one of two today. She wasn't sure she was ready to trade it in for roasted weenies. Moose didn't share her hesitation. "Perfect. The more the merrier. Bring whatever you have."

"Will do." Grandma beamed. "Wait til you see... huh. Lindsay honey, I don't think the oven is doing its job."

Lindsay strode over and held her hands out to the open oven. The turkey inside was pasty and raw. It was lukewarm at best. "Oh no. The heating element must've shorted out." She took out the turkey and put it back in the fridge.

"Well there goes lunch and dinner."

"All the more reason to join us around the campfire," said Moose.

"I know how to fix this," said Lindsay. "I'm going to need to run up north for a part though, and I can't do it with one hand."

Just then, Grace came in with an armful of chopped wood. She set it down by the back door and joined them at the stove. "Why are we all looking in the oven?"

"It's busted," said Grandma.

"I'm going to run out right now. We'll have it fixed in no time," said Lindsay.

"I'll help you when you get back." Grace retrieved her bundle of wood and carried it into the living room.

"I'll grab those roasting sticks for you before I leave," Lindsay told Moose. She headed outside, pulling on her nubbly hat and mittens. The camping gear was under a tarp in the back of the garage. She lifted off the tarp and moved aside two backpacks and a tent.

What was this? She picked up a frame covered in plastic. It was tough to maneuver with her good hand, and she didn't want to drop it or set it on the dirty floor. She carried it to the back door, tapping for someone to let her in. Grandma came to her rescue.

"What do you have there?" she asked.

"I'm not sure," Lindsay replied. "It was mixed in with the camping gear..." She recalled seeing Steve rummaging through it when he picked up his snow blower. Was this connected to him somehow? She carried it into the living room and set it on the couch.

"What's that?" Grace asked.

"I'm not sure, but I have my suspicions..." Lindsay lifted off the plastic to reveal a twin to the painting hanging above them.

Both sisters stepped back, mouths agape.

"Are you thinking what I'm thinking?" asked Lindsay.

"It depends. Where did you find that painting?"

"Hidden in the garage."

"Then yes, yes I am."

Steve was going to switch out the painting

with a fake. They were right. He was never really planning on making amends and…Lindsay gasped.

"What is it?" asked Grace.

"The first day he came back to talk to me, when you were at work and Grandma was here, Steve asked if he could get a picture of Grandma and me on the couch. I thought it was kind of strange, but he seemed to be having a hard time, so I went along with it."

"The painting hung right above you."

"Yes. He was taking a picture of the painting so he could have a copy made." And to think that Lindsay had been even a little bit touched that he'd wanted a picture of her with his "beloved" Grandma Vivian. "He would've stuck around just long enough to switch the paintings and then disappeared again. I'm sure of it."

Grace balled her hands into fists and pursed her lips. "Just when he can't seem to sink any lower, he somehow manages."

"This is great," said Lindsay.

"No it's not. What do you mean?" Grace looked at her sister as though she'd lost her marbles and they'd rolled under the couch, where marbles disappeared and were liable never to be seen again.

"I mean, I'll switch the paintings, put them in each other's frames. We can keep our old family heirloom, and I'll offer Steve his forgery. He can take it right off the wall."

Grace laughed. "That is devious."

"I like to think of it as giving a special gift to someone who has meant so much to me. If it wasn't for him, I might never have known how strong I could be. He's given me enough strength now though, and I'm happy to send him on his merry way."

"Yes. Let's do it right away. I'm not completely confident that he won't sneak in and try to switch the paintings while we're busy over the holidays."

"I'll put the real painting in the safe."

"Well now I almost hope he does sneak in, just so he can steal it."

Lindsay smiled, "We'll see." She switched the frames, hung the fake painting, hid the real one upstairs, and went to the hardware store to get a new element for the oven. When she returned over an hour later, a campfire was blazing in the back yard next to the orchard and Brian and Grandma were standing around it, warming their hands.

"Hey girlie, we've got the fire going. Just waiting for you to get roasting," Grandma yelled.

"I'll be right over. I'm going to fix the oven and pop the turkey in."

Lindsay went inside and found Grace and Officer Anselme kissing under the mistletoe. She closed the door a little harder than was strictly necessary and they jumped apart. Stifling a laugh, Lindsay said, "Hi Dave. Long time no see."

Dave gurgled something about Merry Christmas and sat down at the table.

Grace took the heating element from Lindsay's hand and rubbed Dave's shoulder. "Don't worry. Lindsay's not as protective of me as I let on. In fact, it's often the other way around."

You're telling me, Lindsay thought. "We can look out for ourselves from here on out," she said to her sister, giving her a pointed look.

"Yeah, I think that's about right," Grace said. She waited until Lindsay's had turned away to say, "We have each other's backs though."

Lindsay sighed. "Sometimes we do. Yes. To a reasonable extent."

Dave listened to them with perplexity written all over his face, clearly getting the feeling he was missing something. He was, but neither of the sisters would ever tell him what that something was.

Lindsay changed the subject, saying, "I was really excited when Grace told me that you'd be here today. We haven't seen much of each other in an unofficial capacity."

He smiled. "I hear you have some pretty specific traditions. I'm just trying to keep up."

"We checked off Christmas market and sledding," Grace added.

"And kissing under the mistletoe can be checked twice." Lindsay couldn't resist.

"Oh at least," Grace said.

Dave hid his face in his hands then laughed. "Cut me a break. I'm the new guy here."

"Sorry," Grace said. "You're just too cute when you blush. I promise to be a good sport when I meet your four brothers. Four! Can you believe it?" Grace asked Lindsay. "And all older."

"They look out for me too," Dave said, "but I know they'll give us a hard time. They're all married with kids, and they're always teasing me about being the last man standing. Actually, you'll be the first girlfriend I bring home for Christmas."

"Ooh. I'm flattered, but a little nervous. I promise not to tease you anymore."

"Nah, go for it," he said. "I can handle it."

"Do you guys have any traditions I need to know about?"

"Hmm...well, we don't have a list like you do, but yeah, we have some traditions."

"Ooh. Like what?" Grace had that Christmas gleam in her eye again.

"You aren't going to make another list, are you?"

"I can't make any promises."

"Fair enough. I'll tell you anyway. My dad is obsessed with his grill. He'll be outside grilling hamburgers and chicken for lunch. Also, we have a fireplace in the basement. The kids play down there, and it always smokes us out every year, without fail. The kids have to run upstairs while Dad leaves the grill and curses at the fireplace. Don't worry though, he always fixes it."

Grace laughed. "Couldn't he just do that in advance?"

"He does, and it works fine the rest of the year. We're fairly certain it's possessed. I always leave smelling like smoke. It's the smell of the holidays. Also, one of my brothers sleds down the hill in the backyard in his boxers."

Now it was Lindsay's turn to laugh. "Why?"

"One year when he was in high school some friends dared him to, and he did. It's actually funnier now that he's forty-plus. One of his kids went with him last year, and they sent a video to a few of his old buddies."

"I can't wait. It sounds like a blast."

"Do you two want a hand with that?" Dave asked, getting up from his chair.

Grace was leaning inside the oven, unscrewing the old heating element. "Thanks, but we've got this," she said. "Let's get to work." The sisters had the old element out and the new one installed in no time. The oven heated up, the turkey went back in, and all was well in their world once more. "We're amazing," said Grace. "The snow blower's up next."

"You want to help me with that?" Lindsay asked, surprised.

"I would love to. Figuring out how to do all of this stuff is way too much fun."

Lindsay knew what she needed to do now, and she had all of the parts. If she had another set of hands, they'd be unstoppable. If only her great-grandma could see them now.

"Are you staying for the weenie roast?" Lindsay asked Dave.

"I wouldn't miss it," he said.

All three of them joined Grandma and the Sasquatch hunters at the fire. Grace handed out mugs of steaming cider then burnt her hot dog to a crisp and ate it plain, just the way she liked it. They talked and laughed like old friends, and Lindsay found herself hoping that the hunters would come back again. She remembered the first time she saw them, sloshing a bucket of fish guts on her driveway in their ghillie suits. She hadn't been sure what to expect, other than an unusual few weeks. They had been unusual, there was no doubt about that, but this had turned out to be one of the most memorable months of her life, and they had been a big part of what made it special.

That evening Lindsay, Grandma, and Grace would eat a delicious turkey dinner and then head out to Christmas Eve mass at Saint Mary of the Snows. Brian had asked to accompany them, and of course they were happy to bring him along. Grandma was particularly pleased.

The fire shot sparks into the afternoon sky. Lindsay pronged a hot dog and edged closer to the flames. Her face heated up while the back of her legs stayed chilly. She wondered what Harvey was doing right now, Maddie and James too.

She was clear on who she wanted in her life now: the people who loved her and who she loved right back. Some of them were standing around the campfire that afternoon, but there were three others who were missing and would've made this day complete.

Chapter Twenty-Four

In Which 'Twas the Night Before Christmas

"Lindsay?" Grace tapped on the bedroom door. Lindsay shoved a present under the bed, the last one she still had to wrap, and peeked out.

"What's up?"

"I found this on the front porch." Grace held out a big package. The wrapping paper was silver, not plaid this time, and instead of a tag there was a sticker with her name on it.

"This isn't from you?" Lindsay asked, taking it out of her sister's hand.

"I swear it isn't. I was about to go to bed when I heard someone coming up the driveway. When I looked out the front door, they were pulling away."

"Could you tell who it was?"

Grace nodded.

"Are you going to tell me?"

She shook her head. "Open it first. It'll be a

surprise. The individual who dropped it off must've wanted to be a sneaky monkey."

Again with the sneaky monkey stuff. Lindsay tore open the wrapping paper. She opened the box and peered inside.

"What is it?" Grace asked, craning her neck to get a peek.

"I'm not sure." Lindsay pulled out more of her favorite banana chocolate tea. Nestled in next to it was a big pouch of a strawberry chocolate variety. "I didn't know they even had that."

"Hey, he stole my idea," Grace said. "And he one-upped me."

"So it was a man?"

"Darn...yes it was. But that's all I'm telling you. Is there anything else?"

There *was* something else, and it left Lindsay with no doubt as to who had dropped off the package. It was a little framed picture of two cartoonish characters, a woman and a girl, holding up a basket of cookies and a trophy. It said "winners" above it in fat gold lettering.

There was also a little comic book, its printer paper pages stapled together. It featured two cats named Sunny and Ooper. They were getting ready for Christmas, and it appeared that Ooper was the trouble maker, while Sunny played the straight man. Lindsay chuckled and handed it to Grace. Lindsay and Grace would've loved to have had James in on their stories when they were kids. He had a great sense of humor.

"So, can I ask you about this?" Grace asked. "I've been struggling to hold back, but…"

"You want to ask if you can have some of my tea? No way. It's all mine."

"You know what I mean. What's up with you and Harvey?"

Lindsay set the box full of precious presents on the bed and sat down. Grace joined her.

"You were right," said Lindsay. "Harvey tried to kiss me the night of the bake-off."

Grace didn't seem surprised at all. "Yeah. I saw that coming a mile away."

Lindsay laughed and whacked her with a convenient holiday pillow. Some of Grandma's pillows had migrated from the couch to the beds when Brian complained that there was "nowhere to sit on this blasted davenport".

Grace whacked her back. These pillows were turning out to be pretty useful during sister conversations. "Hey, I'm just saying…it was pretty obvious. You said he tried to kiss you. I take it that means he didn't succeed? What got in his way?"

"I did. I told him about Steve coming over to help."

Grace shook her fist in exaggerated outrage. "Blasted Steve!"

"I know. Steve is the ruiner of all good things, but it would've been pretty wrong of me to be making out with Harvey while Steve was still coming over thinking we might get back together. Or, I thought he was thinking that. I guess he was really trying to pull off an art heist. I still can't believe that, by the way."

"I can't either. I keep walking by the painting to make sure it's still there. It really does look identical. Whoever did it was pretty talented."

"I agree, and Steve might have gotten away with it, if we hadn't put two and two together. I never would've suspected that he'd have a forgery made. Is he really that good?"

"No. He's not. It's just hard to imagine that most people don't have some basic level of decency; it is for me anyway. But back to you and Harvey…"

"Okay, back to me and Harvey. I love his family, and he's one of my very favorite people. He's funny and sweet and an amazing dad. He's also one of the kindest people I've ever met. I think I underestimated the value of kindness in my misspent youth."

"So, what's stopping you? Go get him."

"Two things: one is that he was my best friend's husband. Those are her kids. I never considered him that way while she was alive, obviously, and I didn't plan this. I know she would want him to be happy, but would she want him to be with me? That's not an easy question to answer."

Grace looked thoughtful. "I don't think anyone can answer that for sure. Only you know what you're comfortable with. My instinct is to say that she'd be overjoyed that her husband and her friend found un-expected happiness together, but maybe that's just me telling myself what I want to think again, because you're my sister and I want that for you."

"That's what I'm worried about too. That's also why it was so important to me to be really clear on what I wanted for myself before I even thought of taking anything further with Harvey."

"And now you're clear?"

"I'm clear that I would love to be with him."

"I say go for it then."

"I need to think about it."

"You said there were two things," Grace reminded her.

"Yes, the other thing is, I want to prove to myself that I can do this on my own. If I end up with Harvey, I want to be standing on my own two feet. I still feel like I'm faltering."

"You don't want to jump from one guy to another or feel like you're looking for a rescuer."

"Right, or at least, I want to be as certain as possible that I'm not doing that. I'm working on trusting myself to make good choices. What if Harvey is a rebound or if I'm just feeling vulnerable?"

Grace shook her head. "I don't know what to tell you. I think you're right. You need to answer these questions for yourself. I can tell you this though: you can do this on your own, if that's what you choose. You don't always see yourself the way other people see you, so I'm going to keep reminding you that you're way stronger than you realize. You've been keeping this place going, literally singlehandedly now, for months, and everything's going great. We've had some rough patches, but you've figured it out. I think Steve expected you to crumble without him and you haven't. Not even close."

"Thank you. It has been going rather well, but I've had help."

"And that's fine. It's great, actually. Before this happened, you were so closed off about things. I never knew what was going on around here. You were trying so hard to seem content, but it didn't feel genuine. Now, everything has gone a little off the rails from time to time, yes, but I've also seen you happier than you've been in ages. All I have to do is show you that you can trust me and we'll be on our way."

"So you're going to stick around for sure?"

"Yes. I love it here, and we're going to keep making this place even more fabulous than it is already. Have you been out in the barn lately?"

Lindsay had. It looked spectacular, and Grace claimed that it wasn't even close to being finished.

"This New Year's party is going to be the talk of the town," said Grace. She covered a yawn and got up to leave. "See you in the morning. I bet Santa will come." She smiled a sneaky monkey smile and left Lindsay alone with her presents and her thoughts.

Chapter Twenty-Five

In Which Today? Why, it's Christmas Day!

At about the moment when Lindsay was waking up to a sunny and beautiful Christmas morning, all happiness, warmth, and readiness to embrace everything the day had to offer, the creaking of the floorboards outside her bedroom door alerted her to the fact that Grace had just woken up as well. She was undoubtedly creeping towards the living room to slip some additional gifts under the tree. Lindsay took her time stepping into her slippers and wrapping up with her robe. She pulled some gifts of her own out from their hiding places under the bed and in the armoire, leaving a few of them to be delivered later in the day.

She found Grandma, Brian, Moose, and Hook reclining at the kitchen table, laughing and reminiscing about the past two weeks while guzzling festive mugs of thick black coffee. Lindsay scooted by them, hidden behind a towering pile of presents.

"Good morning sunshine," Grandma crowed.

"Hi," Lindsay said. "Merry Christmas. I'll be right back."

As expected, Grace was indeed in the living room, arranging gifts around the tree. She had a way of shimmering around that recalled a fairy godmother, bestowing her blessings with a flick of the wand. Lindsay added her parcels and Grace quickly rearranged everything again so it looked perfect as a picture once more.

"We've expanded our little family compared to last year, wouldn't you say?" Grace asked.

Lindsay agreed. There were a shocking number of gifts under the tree, reflecting the diversity of those who called the inn home for the time being. Some of them were wrapped in brown paper and tied with butcher's twine while others were enveloped with paper chosen by someone, who shall remain nameless but whose name Lindsay could easily guess, with a decidedly adults-only sense of holiday humor.

Back in the kitchen, Lindsay popped the overnight cinnamon rolls in the oven and overheard the guys discussing an ice fishing trip they'd planned for the following morning.

"You're going whitefish fishing?" she asked.

"You bet," said Hook. "Bright and early tomorrow. We've got a guide taking us out on Lake Michigan. Said we'll likely catch our limit in the first couple hours."

"Did you have plans for the fish?"

"Not really, just to eat them. Why? Do you have a special recipe? I've gotta tell you, it's going to be rough on us guys when we leave. We've gotten used to your cooking. Tough to go back to diner and gas station food for a while. If they were all like Emma's Café we'd be alright, but they sure aren't."

"Well, thank you for the compliment," said Lindsay, "and I think you'll love this idea. It's perfect. We can do a fish boil. I haven't done one in ages. Have you ever been to one?"

All three men were listening in; they looked perplexed.

"It sounds kind of strange, but it's really delicious," she assured them.

"Is it a Walloon Belgian thing?" Moose asked. Lindsay's recipes were often inspired by her ancestors, but in this case the tradition hailed from farther north on the peninsula.

"I think it's Scandinavian, actually. It started as a way to feed big groups of loggers, but it's become a popular tourist attraction, because it really is surprisingly delicious."

Moose looked uncertain. "Boiled fish, huh? You just boil it on the stove? This isn't going to be another lutefisk experience is it? Because I've spent enough time in Minnesota to have been there and done that, and I'm not going back."

Lindsay made herself a cup of strawberry chocolate tea (her new second favorite) and joined them at the table. "No. It's nothing like lutefisk. I promise. It's actually cooked outside in a big vat of boiling water. We build a fire under and around it and then drop in a basket of potatoes and onions. When they're almost finished we add a second basket full of fish and a bunch of salt. The salt causes the fat and oil from the fish to rise to the surface, and then we toss a bit of kerosene on the fire for the grand finale. It burns off the fat and leaves you with a really fresh and light tasting fish. It's usually served with a bunch of butter and lemon."

"Let's make a party out of it," Grandma suggested. "It can be a day after Christmas lunch. Invite Harvey and his kids."

That was a tempting idea. Lindsay was going to be bringing presents to them today. She wondered if they would be home this afternoon when she stopped by. She hadn't planned on going over there on Christmas day, but their gifts to her left her feeling emboldened. If they weren't around, she could just leave their presents on the porch, like they had done last night.

"I'll think about asking them. It's a busy time of year, so they may not be available."

"Available, aschmailable. They'll be here. Mark my words."

"They're marked."

"Good. People sometimes forget to mark them, and then credit doesn't go where it's due."

"I never would though."

"I didn't think so, but it doesn't hurt to give a reminder."

The timer beeped on the cinnamon rolls at the same time as the doorbell rang. Grace flew through the kitchen fully dressed, slid across the floor on her holiday socks, and raced out of the room.

Lindsay pulled out the cinnamon rolls and set them on the stove. She piped icing over the lot of them, enough that it collected in the cinnamon and butter filled grooves.

Grace reentered the kitchen with a square jawed, strawberry blonde police officer on her arm.

"Just in time," said Lindsay. "If you like cinnamon rolls, that is."

"It just so happens that I do," said Dave. He joined them at the table, and he and Brian launched into a discussion about a local rascal who had led Brian and his crew on a wild goose chase that terminated in Old Man Carlson's medicinal green house.

When the last of the rolls had been eaten and the dredges of frosting were snitched from the pan, all seven of them went into the living room and gathered around the tree.

"I can't wait," said Grandma, shoving a small square present into Lindsay's lap.

"Aww, thank you." Lindsay pulled open the paper and tossed it on the floor where Joy happily pounced it, shredding it with her back claws. Inside the package was a black and white photo of Great-Grandma Wathelet driving a tractor through a familiar field under a cloudy sky, her hair wrapped in a white kerchief. She gripped the steering wheel, peering in front of her in concentration. Another woman stood on the trailer behind the tractor. She perched atop a pile of recently harvested vegetables while two others in tall boots and belted jackets raked the soil around them.

"It's the Women's Land Army," said Grandma. "They're harvesting beets on our farm."

Lindsay couldn't stop staring at it. "I love it. Thank you."

"You're welcome. I had a copy made. There are a lot more where that came from, but this one's my favorite. You can see my mother's determination. And the smile on that woman's face who's standing on the pile of beets! I wonder if she knew they were taking a photo or if she really was having that good a time."

Lindsay handed the picture to Grace. "Your mom looks so much like you," Grace said to Grandma.

"She always was a looker," said Grandma, winking. "She taught me to drive that tractor too; I was pretty good. Your grandpa took over once your dad was born, but I still knew my way around it."

Brian, who had been watching the three women with interest, had gotten up and plucked another gift from beneath the tree. He presented it to Grandma Vivian, who looked surprised but pleased. "For me?" she asked.

"Of course. This has been my favorite Christmas in ages. I had no idea, when we showed up in this sweet little village, that we'd be coming across some of the nicest people we've ever had the pleasure of meeting. I'd be tempted to stay here, if it wasn't for our mission."

Moose and Hook look relieved when he confirmed they'd all be moving on together, not ready to part with their intrepid leader.

Grandma held the gift reverently, taking her

time with the tightly knotted twine. Upon opening it, she gasped. It was a poncho. How had Brian known that royal purple was her favorite color? A brown Sasquatch was knitted across the front.

"Did you make this?" Grandma asked.

"Sure did," said Brian. Bags sagged under his eyes that hadn't been there a few days ago, and Lindsay wondered if he'd acquired them staying up until the wee hours to craft it.

Grandma pulled on the poncho and spun around with her arms out. It fit her perfectly. "It's a treasure."

"Just like you," said Brian. Whoa. This guy was as smooth as fresh linoleum, as Grandma would say.

There was a snicker from his fellows, but Brian quelled it with a look that clearly said, "You two have got a lot to learn, so pay attention."

After all of the presents had been opened and oohed and aahed over, Grace and Dave left for his family celebration up north. Grace practically bounced out of the house. She crossed her fingers at Lindsay before she left and Lindsay crossed hers back. She'd fit in like a missing puzzle piece. Grace was made for big family celebrations. Lindsay couldn't wait to hear her rapturous exclamations over Dave and his family when she got home that evening.

Grandma, Brian, Moose, and Hook visited in the living room, one-upping each other with tales that kept getting taller in proportion to the one that had been told before.

Lindsay told Grandma she was going to run out

for a bit, retrieved three presents from under her bed, and hopped in her car to pay a visit to her other favorite family.

When Lindsay arrived at Harvey's house, she spotted James and Maddie digging a tunnel in a huge snowdrift on the edge of the driveway. James had a shovel, while Maddie opted for the convenience of her mittened hands. Spotting Lindsay before she had come to a stop, Maddie jumped up and slid down the icy slope. She plopped onto her backside and Lindsay gasped, but Maddie was unscathed. She leaped up and ran for the car, arms waving above her head.

"Lindsay!" she called. "Merry Christmas!" Maddie slammed into her, giving her a huge hug.

"Merry Christmas to you."

"Santa came. He even brought me a bag of coal. He left a note that said it wasn't because I'd been naughty, but because Snowman von Snowman told him I wanted some." She looked a little disappointed that she hadn't achieved the necessary naughtiness levels, but maybe she'd start earlier next year, if she thought of it in time.

"Wow. Congratulations. Are you going to make another snowman?"

Maddie considered it. "Yes. But not today. We're making an igloo, and then we're going over to Grandpa and Grandma Jacquemart's."

Lindsay glanced across the street at Maddie's grandparent's farm, Cedar Hollow. It was Bea's farm too. In fact, Bea did the majority of the work now that her parents were getting on in years. The goats weren't out; they must have been in the barn, but a steady white stream of smoke came puffing from the chimney. Their house was nearly identical to hers, a classic two story with red bricks and a bull's-eye window beneath the eaves.

"Did Santa come to your house?" Maddie asked.

"He did," said Lindsay. "He brought me a book."

"Ooh. Me too. I got The Wind in the Willows. What book did you get?"

"The Maltese Falcon."

Maddie nodded her head in approval and ran back to the igloo.

"Hi Lindsay!" James called, sticking his head out from the snow cave. "Want to check out our fort?"

Lindsay scooped up their presents from the back seat and headed over to check it out.

"It's warm in here," said James. He climbed out and shook the snow off his knees. Lindsay peeked inside.

"Impressive," she said. "Are you planning on tunneling all the way through?"

"Yeah. Maddie's working on the other side."

"Very cool, guys. I'm going to run inside and say hi to your dad, but then I'll come back out to help you. If you want my help, that is."

"We do!" said Maddie, climbing back up the side of the snow pile to carry on with her project.

Although Lindsay had knocked on Harvey's front door countless times, her heart fluttered as she walked around the house and climbed the stairs. She tapped tentatively at first, but the door swung open immediately.

"That was quick," she said, as Harvey let her inside.

"I saw you out with the kids," he said. "Come on in." The house was warm and smelled like a combination of Christmas tree, waffles, and bacon: the scents of a happy Christmas morning.

Lindsay set the presents on the floor, and Harvey took her coat and hung it in the closet. "Can you stick around a while?"

"I'd love to. Maddie said you're heading over to your parents' soon."

"In about an hour, but that gives us some time. I'm so happy you came by…" he reached out to hug her then stopped, as if catching himself. They stood in the entryway looking at each other, then glancing away and looking anywhere else.

"Hey, Merry Christmas," Harvey finally said, fiddling with the buttons on the ends of his red and black checkered flannel. He still avoided her gaze.

"Merry Christmas to you too."

"Did you have a good morning?" he asked.

"It was great," Lindsay said. She filled him in on her Christmas morning activities. "I hear Maddie got her coal."

"She did. It was her favorite thing. Santa should've just brought her a huge sack of the stuff." They both laughed then went back to glancing around in silence.

"Can I say something?" Harvey asked.

"Of course."

"Okay. I hope it was alright to bring you those presents last night. I know we said we were going to take some time from each other, give one another some space, but I thought about it more, and I just don't know."

"I loved the presents. They were perfect. It was so sweet of you all to think of me. The kids' drawings were my absolute favorite things. Also, I tried the strawberry chocolate tea this morning, and it's right up there with the banana. I'll have to bring some over so I can have it here too."

"You will? Oh. That's great. Yeah. That's what I was wondering about. I thought about it more, like I said, and I don't think it's right for us not to spend time together, unless that's what you want of course."

Lindsay was tempted to break out in the Hallelujah Chorus, but she refrained, not wanting to freak him out. "I agree. We've always been friends. There's no need for that to change."

He smiled and looked at her directly now. "Exactly. You're still figuring things out, and that might take you a long time; I know that, but no matter what you decide, we'd love to have you in our life, in whatever way that ends up working out."

"Thank you. That means a lot to me. I feel the same way about you guys. I really missed you."

"I missed you too...I mean, we did. We all missed you, but I missed you. I..." He chuckled. "You know what I mean."

"I missed you too," she said.

"Do you want to come all the way in? We don't need to stand in the doorway the whole time." Lindsay followed him into the kitchen, and they sat down at the table.

"I wasn't planning on saying anything about it today," said Lindsay, "but since it's come up...Steve and I are getting divorced. I called him the other day and let him know that it was the right thing for me. I've known that for a long time, but..."

Maddie slammed the back door and stomped into the kitchen with her boots on, leaving a trail of stiff snow zigzags behind her.

"Hey buddy, take your boots off on the mat," said Harvey. Lindsay scanned his face for a reaction to her news, but he looked like he always did: unruffled and content.

"I'm just checking if Lindsay's coming out. She's been in here forever." Maddie said, grabbing Lindsay's hand and trying to pull her out the door.

"Just a second. I don't have my coat." Lindsay took it out of the closet and jogged back into the kitchen. "Got it. Don't expect the fort building expertise I showed pre-wrist break though."

"I won't," Maddie assured her. "You're in recovery. You coming, Dad?"

"I'll be right out," he said.

By the time Maddie and Lindsay got back outside, shuffling across the driveway to the hidden snow cave, James had just broken through to the other side of the tunnel and was digging so furiously that all they could see was a steady stream of snow flying from behind the hill.

Maddie peeked in the opposite side. "You did it! I can see you." She cupped her hands around her mouth like a megaphone and yelled, "Hello over there."

"This is awesome," said James, emerging from the cave. His formerly black hat was so snow covered it had turned white. "You guys want to dig on that side?"

"Sure," said Lindsay. She eyed up the hole, trying to judge if it was wide enough for her to enter without getting wedged inside.

Maddie had no such concerns. She jumped in headfirst as Harvey came out the back door.

"Whoa. Nice work guys," he said, sticking his head inside the cave, his voice echoing within the tunnel. "It's way bigger than it looks from the outside."

"Do you want to come in?" Maddie asked from within.

"I'm going to pass."

"Is it because you're claustrophobic?"

"That's part of it."

"What's the other part?"

"I'd probably get stuck like when Pooh visits Rabbit."

"Ha!" Maddie said. "That would be so funny. We could use your butt as a table."

"Funny for you maybe."

Maddie's laughter, accompanied by a couple of snorts rang out from inside the tunnel.

James hopped onto the driveway with his shovel. "Is it almost time to go over to Grandpa and Grandma's?"

Harvey pulled out his phone and checked the time. "Just about."

"I'd better run," said Lindsay, "but I have an invitation for you three. It's a last minute idea, so I understand if you have something else going on." She'd been nervous about asking them to come over, but after their conversation in the house, it seemed like exactly the right thing to do.

"We'll be there," said Maddie, who had emerged from her cave once more.

"Don't you want to hear what it is first?" Lindsay asked.

"Nah, you always do fun things."

"Why thank you," said Lindsay. "Here's the plan: our lodgers..."

"AKA the Bigfoot hunters," said James.

"Yes, AKA the Bigfoot hunters, are going ice fishing tomorrow morning, and we're having a fish boil for lunch. Interested in joining us?"

James and Maddie looked to their dad with wide pleading eyes. "I don't know..." he said.

"Come on, Dad," said James. "It's a fish boil! Also, we'll get to meet the Bigfoot hunters. I'm going to interview them for my next graphic novel. Wouldn't that be cool?"

"That would be really cool," said Harvey. "Of course we can go. I can't wait."

"Yes!" said the kids together.

Yes, thought Lindsay.

It wasn't until she was halfway home that she realized she'd forgotten to give them their presents. Oh well, the gifts would be waiting for them by the door when they got back from their family get-together. She hoped they'd like them.

Grandma Vivian would be back at home waiting for her. They always played Scrabble after lunch on Christmas day. Lindsay would never accuse her grandma of cheating, but she was nearly as creative when it came to inventing words as she was at telling tall tales and got quite belligerent if anyone suggested pulling out a dictionary or checking a phone to verify if her words were legitimate.

Last Christmas runkle was a disputed word, one that Grandma insisted she'd been using for ages and if the dictionary said otherwise, one of them was wrong and it wasn't her. For the past twelve months she'd been casually slipping it into her sentences, but its meaning remained elusive. It was adaptable. It could be used as a noun, verb, or adjective (runkly).

Lindsay wondered what this year's word would be. She also wondered what other novelties the new year would bring.

Chapter Twenty-Six

*In Which a Fish Boil and Some Cherry Pie
Will Help to Make the Season Bright*

"Stand back," said Lindsay. "I'm pouring on the kerosene."

"Should you be doing that?" asked Grandma. "Here, let me." Grandma attempted to take the container, but instinct told Lindsay that doing this with her left hand was safer than giving Grandma free reign to try it with either.

After a bit of a dance, Grandma gave up and edged away from the boiling pot along with everyone else as Lindsay sprinkled kerosene on the fire. It flared to three times its original size, letting off a wave of heat before dying back down, and Grace and Dave lifted the baskets out of the water, lugging them to the driveway so they could scoop out the delicacies inside.

Everyone gathered in the kitchen and enjoyed their feast around the table. James was shy about talking to Brian at first, but once they got started, the curious author asked rapid-fire questions, pulling out a notebook and jotting down ideas for his next comic book. Brian regaled him with tales of thrilling adventures and exciting near-misses.

Harvey sat next to Lindsay, and she found herself being unusually aware of his every movement. He rubbed that red spot next to his cuticle on his right thumb like he sometimes did when he was anxious. He picked the fish away from its delicate bones and lifted it to his mouth then savored it, licking his butter covered lips.

They had to squish close together, because there were so many people at the table, but he seemed to be even closer to Lindsay than the situation warranted. There was plenty of room on his other side, between him and Grace. His shoulder brushed Lindsay's and he glanced her way.

"You have something in your hair," he said, reaching up and disentangling a pine needle from a curl near her temple. He smelled like the soft white heat of wood smoke from their cooking fire, like the warm musky coconut of his shampoo, the same scent that had filled his bathroom the day Lindsay came upon him stepping out of the shower. He removed the needle slowly and gently, and, without meaning to, her mind went back to the day he tried to kiss her and color rose to her cheeks.

"Thanks," she said. "That must've happened when I was watering the tree. It's starting to dry out."

"Your house looks really festive. You guys went all out this year," he said.

"That was Grandma's doing," Lindsay replied, looking over at her grandma, who darted her eyes away before she could be caught staring at them.

"Are you coming to the New Year's party?" Grace asked Harvey, leaning over her plate to direct her question at Lindsay as well.

"Oh, I'm not sure. My parents offered to watch the kids..." he said

"You should go, Dad," said James.

Maddie looked up from the floor, where she was playing with Joy, to voice her agreement. "Yeah, Grandpa and Grandma will make pizzas and let us drink soda."

Harvey threw up his hands in surrender. "Well in that case, I'd better go."

"It's going to be amazing," said Grace. "Lindsay, you should show Harvey the barn after this. Give him a little sneak preview." Did Grace just wink at her? Lindsay hoped no one else noticed.

"Sure," said Lindsay. "Why don't we go now?" They'd both finished eating, and the kids were still working on their lunches, having been too distracted by the hunters' stories and the rambunctious kitten to focus exclusively on their food.

Lindsay and Harvey stepped outside and crossed the yard side by side to the barn. A swallow sailed overhead followed by another, both swooping towards the orchard. The summer kitchen was still locked, and Lindsay wondered if the hunters were ever going to use their bucket of fish. It was surely still frozen inside. She hoped they planned to take it with them. It still struck her as funny, them driving up to her inn with their bucket of fish in their ghillie suits. She'd never forget that day. It was uncanny, how time changed one's perspective.

If it wasn't for the lodgers and their tireless hunt, Lindsay might never have found the ammo box in the old shed; she might never have discovered the truth about her great-grandfather and may never, in fact, have found the courage to go for the life she truly wanted.

And thinking about the changing filter that the passage of time could drape over one's experiences, Lindsay recalled another day, not too long ago, whose aspect had shifted in light of her new perspective. It was late September, unseasonably warm and muggy, and Maddie and James ran through their backyard in swimsuits, taking turns squirting each other with the garden hose. Harvey and Lindsay lounged in lawn chairs, sipping iced tea and laughing at the kids' gleeful shrieks as they were startled over and over again by the shock of icy water on their sun warmed skin.

Lindsay wrapped her fingers around her tall glass cup, savoring the chill of condensation that had gathered on the outside, and leaned back in her chair, angling her face toward the sun like a sunflower. She opened her eyes, sensing Harvey's gaze.

"I'm trying to figure something out," he said. "Maybe you can help me."

"What's that?"

"Well, there's a job opening at work. My supervisor's encouraging me to go for it, but we'd have to move, and I don't know if I could do that right now."

Lindsay's heart skipped a beat. He couldn't leave. Harvey and his kids had become like family to her, but she couldn't say that. "It would be a huge change for all of you," was all she could manage.

"It would, and my parents are getting up in years. It's been so great living right across the street from them, Bea too." He laughed. "Don't tell her I said that. I didn't mean she's getting old; I meant it's been nice living across the street from her as well."

"I knew what you meant," Lindsay reassured him. He was quite a bit older than Bea, after all, but he didn't need Lindsay to remind him of that.

"I'm ready for something different though-at work, I mean-a new challenge. I've been doing the same thing for a while now. I feel kind of stuck in general, like I'm waiting for something, you know?"

She did know. Oh boy, did she ever. "So you're trying to figure out how to feel unstuck, and maybe taking the job would help with that."

"Maybe, or...it's like, sometimes you think something will make you happy, and you're considering taking a chance with it, but it's a risk too. But if I don't try, I'll never know."

Lindsay drew a sip of her tea. She was probably the last person anyone would want to get advice from about taking risks. She'd been so afraid of change, of rocking the boat, that she'd just let things happen, and here she was. She looked out at the playing kids and the man sitting next to her, waiting for her response. This wasn't such a terrible place to be at all.

She would never have gotten here if Steve hadn't left though; she knew that to be true. Why couldn't something be up to her for a change?

"I don't think you should leave," she said, then immediately felt panic rising in her chest. She should clarify. "Your family means so much to you. It would be hard for you to be apart."

He smiled at her and stood, taking her empty cup. "I don't think I should either. Your opinion is really important to me, though, so thanks."

"Of course," she said.

Back in the present moment, the memory of late summer warmth giving way to winter chill, Harvey and Lindsay stood together inside the barn turned event hall. Harvey whistled as he took in the grandeur of the formerly humble space.

The chandelier was draped in pine boughs. Every rafter was entwined with a garland of evergreen branches, gauzy silver ribbon, fairy lights, and round silver balls. White and silver striped ribbons curled around the wall sconces, which looked like old fashioned gas lanterns. Centered on each round table were massive blue champagne goblets full of silver tinsel and blue and silver baubles.

"You've totally outdone yourselves," he said. "This is unbelievable. Where did you get all those trees?" They stood sentinel around the edges of the room, bedecked to match the garland overhead and the scattered centerpieces.

"Grandma and Lindsay found the spruce screen I planted a while back." Lindsay envisioned her carefully planted hedge, littered with gaping holes like the mouth of a child who'd lost a shocking number of baby teeth in quick succession, and made a mental note to order some new saplings in the spring.

"It's pretty chilly in here," said Harvey. Lindsay was about to explain that they kept the heat turned low when they weren't using the hall, when Harvey pulled his hands out of his pocket and held them up, revealing a pair of thick insulated mittens, "but it's not bothering me at all."

"You got them!"

"Yes, and they're perfect. You made my Christmas."

"I got them from this amazing little shop up north. Did you get your other present?" she asked. "The super secret one that you didn't want to reveal for fear of not getting it?"

"I think I did." He had his back to her; she couldn't see his face, but his tone had changed. Where he had been joking moments before, he was serious now, quieter.

"Well, can you tell me what it is?"

Harvey pretended to be interested in the centerpieces on the table as he said, "I think you might know."

Lindsay was certain that she did. She'd known what he wanted before she even asked, partly because she wanted the exact same thing and partly because of the way he looked at her, the deliberate and tender way he touched her. She crossed the distance between them and took his hand in hers.

"Will you be my date for the New Year's party?" she asked.

"Oh," he said, clearly not expecting the question. His mouth tilted into a half-smile that matched the one she felt forming on her own face. "Yes. Of course I will."

"Perfect." She leaned over and, balancing on one leg, kissed him on the cheek. "Let's go inside. There's cherry pie with ice cream for dessert."

In a daze, Harvey let her lead him back to the house. They strolled down the drive slowly, pulling apart as they reached the door.

"After you," Lindsay said, holding it open for him.

"Thank you," he said, his eyes full of meaning.

"No, thank you" Lindsay replied.

He walked inside and she followed behind.

Chapter Twenty-Seven

In Which Grandma Got Won
Over by a Sasquatch

Lindsay checked the clock on the mantel again. Steve would be there any minute. The warm camaraderie of the fish boil the day before couldn't insulate her from the cold dread she felt now. What if their plan didn't work? What if Steve became suspicious and didn't take the bait?

Grace was stationed outside in the garage, pretending to work on the snow blower but really making sure that Steve didn't try to retrieve his forgery before they'd figured out what to do about the fact that it had mysteriously (for Steve) disappeared. They'd have to figure out how to cover their tracks eventually, but today wasn't going to be that day.

Another minute passed as Lindsay paced in front of the window. She needed to find a way to settle her nerves, but there was no time. Steve was pulling into the driveway. Lindsay took a deep breath. It was natural that she'd be nervous, even without her concerns about the painting. Steve could make her life very difficult if he wanted to, and he'd proven not to have any compunction about doing so, as long as it suited his purposes.

Three raps at the door and Lindsay strode over, as ready as she'd ever be. She swung it open. There was Steve, his face sad and serious. He was playing the part of a man who was crushed at the demise of his marriage, trying to keep a stiff upper lip about the inevitability of it all.

"Come on in," said Lindsay. Steve walked past her solemnly, sat down at the kitchen table, and leaned back in the chair with his ankle over his knee.

His call yesterday evening hadn't been a surprise in the least. Lindsay assumed that he'd want to get things wrapped up as soon as possible, now that he knew it wasn't going to work for him to hang around and bide his time.

Lindsay, who was panicking on the inside, maintained bland, calm indifference on the outside. "Would you like anything to drink?" she asked.

Steve shook his head and looked down sadly. "No thank you. This is going to be tough for both of us, so let's discuss it and get it over with. I would like to propose an idea that I feel is fair."

So he was, in fact, going for the unfortunate and sad separation angle. That was alright. It was what Lindsay had been expecting, more so than the rudeness he'd displayed the previous week. He'd want her to agree to his terms.

Lindsay sat down across from him. "I'd be

happy to consider it. What did you have in mind?"

"Well, I'd like to split our assets 50/50. I'd be open to you buying me out, if you can come up with the cash. This was your family home, and I'm not interested in running the business like you are."

Ha! Lindsay thought. "That does sound fair," she said.

Steve glanced to the side and shrugged his shoulders, as if he was being shy. It was a bit over the top, but it gave Lindsay warning about what was coming next.

"I have a small request though," he said. "I'm afraid it's going to sound kind of silly..."

Lindsay furrowed her brow as if she couldn't imagine what else he might want from little old her.

"You know that painting that's over the couch, the one of the three women?" he asked.

"Sure. It was my great-grandma's. A friend of hers painted it."

"I remember that, yeah. I've always really liked it, and I'm wondering if you might let me have it."

"Oh." *Act surprised and reluctant.* "I don't know..." Lindsay tried not to ham it up too much, "it has sentimental value."

"I know it does, and that's why I feel awkward asking, but it's grown to mean a lot to me too. It'll be a memento of our time together, of what we were once upon a time."

Lindsay resisted the urge to gag. "You'll always have your memories. Do you really need the painting too?" She couldn't give in too easily. She tried to imagine how she would respond if he was asking for the real painting; she'd be hesitant to give it up.

"I don't *need* it, but you're the one who is choosing to end our marriage, and it would mean so much to me."

"I can see that. I think I can agree to those terms." Would it be terribly suspicious if she got up and did a jig?

"Thank you. It's awful that our marriage didn't survive this storm, just awful, but I know we'll carry on separately somehow. I'm actually moving away, heading out to California to start over. Too many memories here..."

"You always wanted to move out there. That's great. Good for you. I'm so sorry it didn't work out between us."

"Me too," Steve said. "Maybe I shouldn't ask, but just in case, would it be alright if I took the painting now? I'd hate for you to have to ship it to me later. We can file for divorce and handle the financial stuff from a distance."

Lindsay nodded. Now she was the one struggling to act crestfallen. "You can take it. I hope it's some consolation for our joint loss."

A smirk, just the ghost of one, rose up on his face before being overpowered by sheer force of will into a rueful frown. "It'll help, sure. Well, I guess this is goodbye."

"Goodbye."

She stood, following him into the living room, where the picture, still decked out with a golden strand of garland, had pride of place above the pillow strewn couch. Lindsay pulled off the garland and, lifting the painting off the wall, handed it to Steve.

Was it her imagination, or had his eyes given off a golden spark, like the eyes of a dragon surveying its hoard? It was probably her imagination, but regardless, he accepted the heirloom solemnly and assured her once again that he would think of her whenever he gazed upon it. He was laying it on a tad thick now, but it wouldn't be much longer and he'd be on his way. Lindsay only had to keep the charade going for another ten minutes, tops.

He must've been tiring of it too, because he said, "Take care," and patted her arm.

"You too," she said, patting him back.

She walked him to the door then watched him from the window. He peeked in the garage, spotted Grace, and nonchalantly strolled to his truck with the painting, which he placed on the passenger seat. He backed out of the driveway and rolled out of sight.

Lindsay met Grace in the garage.

"So..." said Grace.

Lindsay couldn't hide her elation anymore. She beamed at her sister. Steve had gone for it, and he was moving about as far away as he could get without leaving the country.

Grace cheered. "You did it. I knew you could. Tell me everything."

Lindsay recounted their entire conversation as they walked back to the house. "How much do you bet I'll get a text saying he had a copy made for me and left it in the garage?"

"Oh, that's a guarantee. He's not going to want you to run across it, and as a bonus he'll get to bolster the illusion of what a thoughtful guy he is."

"If only…"

Before they reached the back door, Grandma and Brian drove up in his truck.

Grandma had a story of her own to share. She launched out of the truck and started right in on it. "Ladies, I'm going to miss you, but Brian's asked me to accompany him on his next adventure, and I said yes."

Lindsay wasn't shocked by this news, and from the look on her face, neither was Grace.

Grandma was taken aback, clearly anticipating a different response. "Oh, come on. I thought you two would be knocked off your rockers. Here I am, your little old Grandma, and I'm off on a cross country hunt."

"I've never thought of you as my little old Grandma," said Grace, echoing Lindsay's thoughts exactly.

Grandma huffed. "What do you mean? I'm little, I'm old, and I'm your Grandma. What's left for a lady to do when she can't surprise people anymore?"

"I think you've answered your own question," said Lindsay. "You go on a Sasquatch hunt with a handsome safari man."

Grandma nodded appreciatively. Lindsay had a point. "Alright, you win."

Brian joined them, putting his arm around Grandma's shoulder. "Don't worry, I'll take good care of Vivian here."

"Bah. More like I'll be taking care of you," Grandma replied.

Brian conceded. "We'll take care of each other."

"When will you be leaving?" asked Lindsay. They were supposed to be staying for three more nights.

"We thought about heading out tomorrow," said Grandma. "That way we could head down to Florida and spend New Year's with your parents." So she must've come clean about her grandparent status. That was reassuring to hear.

"We'll also be on the trail of the skunk ape in Big Cypress National Preserve," said Brian. "He's the Florida version of Bigfoot. His distinctive odor might be an asset when we're tracking him down."

"That's right," said Grandma. "We'll be tromping through saw grass, fleeing alligators and giant snakes, and leaping over patches of quicksand."

It didn't sound like a good time to Lindsay, but Grandma was beside herself with excitement.

"You can keep the fish bucket," said Brian, magnanimously donating the relic of their time together to a not-all-that grateful innkeeper. "Skunk apes are partial to lima beans. We'll rustle some up on our way."

"Thanks," said Lindsay. It wasn't all bad news; she could use the fish as fertilizer in the spring.

"Don't worry about us, either," said Grace. "We'll be doing just fine, although I don't know how we would've gotten through this month without you."

"It was my pleasure. What a wild ride, right?" asked Grandma.

She wasn't kidding. "More good news," said Lindsay. She told Grandma about the outcome of her meeting with Steve, minus the part of the agreement that led him to take his own forged painting.

"Well, I didn't expect him to go softly, but hey, we'll take it, right? Goodbye Steve, hello the rest of your life. Wahoo!" Grandma skipped up the stairs and went inside.

"You're going to have your hands full," Grace informed Brian.

"I wouldn't have it any other way," he said.

"Neither would we," said Grace. Lindsay agreed wholeheartedly. Grandma was priceless.

Chapter Twenty-Eight

In Which a New Year Brings New Hope

"What do you think?" Grace asked. She twirled in pointy silver flats, the black satin skirt of her dress flaring and twisting around her, black lace sleeves skimming delicate wrists. She paused, taking in Lindsay's appearance for the first time. "Whoa. Look at you!"

Now it was Lindsay's turn to twirl. Smoothing her shiny gold skirt she said, "I'd say we're both ready for a fabulous New Year's party."

"With fabulous dates. I still can't believe you and Harvey are going together. It's too good to be true."

"I'm definitely going to have to agree with you there. I'm in shock, myself." Lindsay had gotten ready this morning in a half-daze, not daring to feel too confident that the day would go even half as well as it was shaping up to be. So far, though, everything had gone without a hitch. The hall looked lovely, the food was prepared, and now she and Grace were outfitted and ready to host.

"Did you hear from Grandma this afternoon?" Grace asked as they headed into the kitchen. "I thought I heard you talking to her."

"I did. I forgot to pass along the message to you. She says she's having a wonderful time on the beach beneath the palm trees with Brian, and they're going to be watching fireworks tonight, but after that the skunk ape hunt is on. Also, Mom and Dad say hello."

"Nice. I can't wait to see Grandma's pictures. I wonder if she'll be coming back any time soon."

"Me too. It's not the same around here without her."

"Maybe we need to start ramping up our energy level," said Grace. "It's pretty hilarious that it's gotten weirdly quiet with the departure of our grandma."

"Careful what you wish for."

"What do you mean?"

"I mean you might want to enjoy the peace while it lasts. We have another group coming next week, and I have a sneaking suspicion they might be in the same vein as our most recent lodgers."

Grace looked at Lindsay, waiting for her to admit that she was pulling her leg. When no such admission came, Grace said, "Alright. Bring 'em on." She flipped on the radio, which still played holiday music, and danced to the fridge, where a bowl of punch sat chilling on the top shelf. She lifted it out then slowed her sashay to a shimmy as the punch swayed along, testing the strength of its cellophane boundaries.

"See you out there," Grace called, edging open the door. Lindsay grabbed a tray of barbecue chicken roll-ups and followed her out to the barn.

Inside the event hall, the heat was up, the scent of pine wafted through the air, lights blazed from trees and lanterns, and music poured from overhead speakers. All they needed were their guests, who would be arriving at any moment, and the evening would be complete.

"Auld lang syne," Grace said, musing, as the song came on. "Funny how I've heard it so many times, but I've got no idea what it means. When I was a kid I thought it was 'Old Lang Sign.'"

Lindsay set down her tray and rearranged the food on the table. "It does sound like that. It means old long since in Scottish Gaelic."

"Old long since?"

"Days gone by."

"How do you know that?"

"I've always loved that song. It's by Robert Burns, the Scottish poet. You know, 'My love is like a red, red rose...'"

"Yes! 'And I will love thee still, my dear, till a' the seas gang dry.' Grandma used to read that to us."

"She did, didn't she? Along with Keats, and Shelley, and Byron. Do you think she was trying to turn us into a couple of romantics in her image? Dad's so serious. Maybe we were her second chance."

Grace laughed. "I don't doubt that's true, and it worked, in a roundabout way. Hey, let's have a romantic night, one where we don't worry about anything. It'll be in honor of Grandma, and this month, and days gone by, and just everything that's happened this year."

"I'm already on it," said Lindsay, turning away from her sister and back to the table in order to hide the grin spreading across her face.

"Are you up to something?" Grace asked, walking around so they were facing each other once more.

Lindsay shrugged, but the glint of mischief in her eye must have been obvious to Grace, who possessed her own glint often enough for her to recognize it when she came across it in someone else.

"What is it?" Grace asked, but she was met with another shrug. "Is it going to happen tonight?"

"Yes. Whatever it is, you won't have long to wait."

"Will you at least give me a clue?"

"Nope...hey, it's Bea and Wes." The first guests to arrive at their last event of the year rescued Lindsay from the temptation to reveal her scheme.

"This place looks incredible," said Bea, echoing the refrain that would pop up over and over later that evening.

"Why, thank you," said Grace. "I'm not finished bugging you," she whispered to Lindsay as an aside, in case Lindsay had any doubt in her mind about whether her sister was going to let it go.

Lindsay made her escape to greet more of their guests, while Bea and Wes grabbed hors d'oeuvres and sat down at a table with Grace. People poured into the hall: close friends, neighbors, and those that Lindsay rarely saw from around the village clustered in groups laughing, dancing, and eating.

Chloe and Arthur arrived a bit late, bearing an ergonomically sound wheel barrow.

"How thoughtful of you two. Is this to wheel me out at the end of the night?" Lindsay asked.

"You got it," said Chloe. "I assumed you'd be letting loose tonight, now that your visitors are gone, and thanks to my excellent design capabilities Grace's back will suffer no ill effects the next morning from hauling your weight."

"Seriously though, this looks like a well thought out piece of equipment," said Lindsay, scoping out its curved handles and deep bucket.

"Yeah," said Arthur. "I've been using one on my farm and it's really something." Lindsay would take his word for it. She couldn't wait to try it out.

"Maybe I should take this out to your garage. It's a little out of place here," said Chloe. They were starting to attract some funny looks.

"I can take it," said Lindsay. She needed to go out to check on something and didn't want anyone else to come upon her surprise before it was ready. She rolled the wheel barrow out the door and towards the garage. There was no sign of Harvey or her neighbor, who would be coming over any minute.

She deposited the wheel barrow in the garage and paused to take a look at her snow blower, which was working like a charm. The real test had been when it snowed last night, filling Lindsay with a nameless dread that stemmed from the fact that, as previously mentioned, the higher the stakes, the lower the likelihood that the machine would deign to start. This morning, however, she fired it up with nary a hiccough and cleared the driveway with time to spare for a second cup of strawberry chocolate tea.

The smooth sailing had been the culmination of a week of hard work. She and Grace learned more about auger transmissions, scraper bars, belts, and fuel stabilizers than they'd ever dreamed possible. (They hadn't dreamed about it at all previously, so it didn't take much, but Lindsay was quite proud of all they'd accomplished.)

She gave it one last appreciative glance then stepped out of the garage just as Harvey was coming up the drive. In dark jeans and a chunky cardigan, he cleaned up really nice. When he spotted her, he stopped and smiled as if to say, "Well, here we are."

She crossed the driveway in her heels until she reached him.

"Happy..." Harvey began.

Lindsay placed her finger over his lips then caressed his face with her hand, just as he had done what felt like ages ago. There it was again: the scent of his coconut shampoo. It mingled with the smoky spice of home made pizza this time. Running her hand around to the back of his head, she tangled her fingers in his hair and they kissed, finally, right there in the middle of the driveway.

Flurries tumbled about around them, flashing in the light coming from the barn before being swallowed up by the darkness once more.

"Happy New Year's," said Lindsay.

"I'd say," Harvey replied, kissing her again. She was elated, soaring, and certain that she'd never been kissed like this before. Harvey took her hand and they ambled towards the lights and sounds of the party. "If I'd known I was going to be greeted like that, I'd have gotten here sooner. Sorry I was late, by the way. I walked the kids over to my parents' house, and they begged me to stay for a slice of pizza."

"No worries," said Lindsay. "You got here right on time…" She glanced behind her and spotted someone else coming up the drive whose arrival she'd also been anticipating. "Speaking of perfect timing, I have someone stopping by right now. Want to meet me inside?"

"Sure," said Harvey, slipping through the door. Lindsay turned around. Her neighbor Jack was trotting up the driveway with Mimi, his Belgian draft horse. Lindsay waved them over to the side of her garage, where the sleigh was waiting in the shadows to make its debut after years of disuse.

"Do you want help harnessing her up?" Lindsay asked. She greeted Mimi with a stroke of her mane.

"No thanks. I've got it," said Jack, dismounting. "Are you going to be alright driving the sleigh? She's used to it, but I know it's been a few years for you."

"I think I'll be alright," said Lindsay, but she was starting to feel a bit nervous. Between the massive weight of the sleigh, her broken wrist, and the immense power of the horse, she'd need to have her wits about her.

"It'll come back to you. Remember, it's all about communicating your confidence, and I'll be right inside if you need me. Once you have the first ride, I'll take over from there."

Confidence. Lindsay had that. She could do this. "I'll be right back," she said.

"Sounds great. She'll be ready and raring to go."

Inside the barn, Lindsay scanned the crowd. Wes and Bea danced away out on the dance floor. Chloe and Arthur sat at a table, talking animatedly together. They were always laughing. Grace and Dave were slow dancing beneath a huge clump of mistletoe that Lindsay recognized as a transfer from their kitchen. Grace must've sneaked that in at the last minute, because it hadn't been there yesterday when they were putting on the finishing touches. Viva la Grandma.

There was Harvey, talking with a group of friends at a table in the back. Lindsay walked up behind him, putting her hand on his shoulder. "Hey guys, I hate to interrupt," said Lindsay, "but there's someone who needs Harvey outside."

Harvey looked at her with another one of his tilted grins and they headed back out into the quiet night. "What are you up to?" he asked.

"I have a little surprise for you."

"You didn't have to do that. I already got what I really wanted." He wrapped his arm around her waist and pulled her close.

"So did I, but this will be a fun extra."

They rounded the corner; the nearly full moon shone down upon a one horse open sleigh.

"She's all yours," said Jack, stepping aside as Lindsay climbed aboard, pulled a woolen blanket over her legs, and took the reins in her hand.

Harvey stood there in shock. "This is incredible. Please never tell Maddie that we got to do this and she didn't."

"Come on up," said Lindsay. When Harvey was ensconced beside her, she said, "Maddie can have a ride soon, too. Jack and I are teaming up. He's going to use my sleigh and charge my guests for winter sleigh rides."

"And you'll get to have a horse around here again," said Harvey.

"Yes. Isn't it perfect? She's beautiful." Mimi shook her mane in agreement and the sleigh bells around her neck jingled.

"How do you get her to go?"

"I say, 'Mimi, walk.'" Mimi edged forward right away and the sleigh glided across the powdery snow through the illuminated field. The sound of the sleigh gliding along mingled with the merry jangling of the bells. They flew passed the dark woods, tucking their chins against the whistling wind.

Harvey put his arm around Lindsay's shoulders.

"Do you want to take the reins?" she asked him. "You need to hold on tight."

"I'll try." He disentangled his arm and took over. "How were you doing this with only one good wrist?" he asked. "It takes a lot of strength."

"I've had practice," said Lindsay.

When they got to the edge of the field, Mimi stopped and Harvey relinquished the reins. They glided back to the barn, where Jack was waiting for them.

"How'd it go?" he asked.

"Fantastic," said Lindsay. "Thank you for doing this. Everyone will love it."

"Hey, thank you. I'm looking forward to getting back into giving sleigh rides. Mimi is too. Do you want to send more people out?"

Lindsay and Harvey went back to the barn where Lindsay filled Grace in on what was waiting outside. "You can pick another couple to go with you."

Grace, who had been beaming a moment before, stared at the entrance with a look of shock on her face and said, slowly, "Like Betsy and George?"

"What?" Lindsay whipped around to see that very couple striding towards them.

"Hey guys," Betsy said.

"Look whose back, right?" said George, pulling off his completely unnecessary sunglasses and sliding them into the pocket of his impeccably tailored tux.

Lindsay scrambled to hide her surprise. "Oh. Hi guys. Happy New Year. So good to see you. Long time no see." She needed to stop rambling.

Grace jumped in to save her. "Would you two be interested in taking a sleigh ride with Dave and me?"

"That sounds perfect." Betsy grabbed George's arm and pulled him back out the door. Grace followed behind with Dave, glancing back at Lindsay with a look that clearly stated, "Yeesh."

"Well, that was unexpected," said Harvey.

"You're telling me," Lindsay agreed.

"Do you think Arthur knows?"

"He does now." Across the room, Arthur scowled at the spot where his brother had just stood while Chloe whispered in a steady stream beside him. Lindsay was concerned for Betsy-and Chloe for that matter-but there was nothing she could do about it tonight. In the spirit of romance, she took Harvey's arm and they waltzed each other out onto the dance floor.

They danced the slow songs and the fast ones while couple after couple came in and out of the barn to take their turn on the sleigh. Wes and Bea joined them on the dance floor, and Wes dropped to one knee.

"Not again," Lindsay thought. She almost teased him about it, but he was staying down there too long. He wasn't tying his shoe this time, and he wasn't getting up either. He reached into his pocket. More chocolate Santas? No, it was a box.

Bea, noticing his tell-tale pose this time, stopped dancing. Her hands flew to her mouth and tears sprung to her eyes as Wes flipped opened the velvet box. People all around them stopped dancing as well, looking on.

"Bea," said Wes. "I love you. I've known that

you were the one for me since the day we met. You're kind and beautiful and smart and you can out-milk anyone, and I would be honored if you would agree to spend the rest of your life with me."

He stood and Bea flew into his arms. She kissed him, tears streaming down her face now. "Yes!" she cried, and everyone around them cheered, Lindsay the loudest.

"I hope you have an opening for a wedding this summer," Bea called to her.

"You bet," said Lindsay, who surprised herself by crying as well.

As midnight approached, Lindsay got ready for the count-down and prepared to play the customary song, the one with the words by Robert Burns. Everyone was inside now, even Jack, who had taken Mimi home for the evening and returned for the festivities.

As the countdown began, Harvey took Lindsay's hands in his.

Five...Wes and Bea shared a straw bale, admiring the ring that had been his grandmother's.

Four...Betsy and George whispered in a corner beside a glowing Christmas tree.

Three...Dave and Grace spun across the dance floor.

Two...Chloe and Arthur snapped on shiny hats and squeaked metallic blowers.

One.

"Happy New Year!" everyone shouted. Lindsay pulled Harvey close, and they kissed, neither realizing that they stood right beneath Grace's big clump of mistletoe. So Lindsay could cross it off the list for herself too, after all.

Author's Note

Although the people and many of the specific places in this tale come entirely from my imagination, Namur, Wisconsin is a real town and a little known National Historic Landmark in Southern Door County. It is nestled at the base of a peninsula that separates the waters of Green Bay and Lake Michigan. In the mid-1800s, Belgian immigrant families from the French speaking region of Wallonia settled the area, and it remains one of the longest-standing immigrant enclaves in the United States. The red brick farmhouses, roadside chapels, and summer kitchens still dot the landscape, and the local delicacies are on display every year at the Kermiss harvest festival.

My favorite part of writing, other than getting to spend time with my funny characters, is hearing from readers. Please consider leaving a review of Christmas at Cherry Bounce Inn on Amazon. All feedback is appreciated, as it helps me grow as a writer and will help direct others to a series that they may enjoy as well. Thank you so very much and Merry Christmas!

Acknowledgements

Many thanks to Margie and Mary for your invaluable editorial assistance. Any and all errors are my own, but your attention to detail has made this a better book and is very much appreciated. As always, thank you to Joe for being my first reader and laughing at the parts where you knew I was cracking myself up. Thank you for being my leading man and providing both inspiration and banana chocolate tea. To EMF: thank you for crafting the plot twist late into the night and laughing until we cry about this story and all the others. Last but certainly not least, thank you to everyone who has read my books and encouraged me along the way. If a book is a conversation, I'm thrilled to have been gifted this time with each and every one of you.